SWITCH

SWITCH

Carol Snow

HARPERTEEN
An Imprint of HarperCollins*Publishers*

HarperTeen is an imprint of HarperCollins Publishers.

Switch
www.harperteen.com

Library of Congress Cataloging-in-Publication Data
Snow, Carol.
Switch / Carol Snow. — 1st ed.
    p. cm.
Summary: Fifteen-year-old Claire discovers that, like her long-dead but very much
present grandmother, she has the ability to inhabit other bodies while asleep.
ISBN 978-0-06-145208-6 (trade bdg.)
[1. Supernatural—Fiction. 2. Identity—Fiction. 3. Grandmothers—Fiction. 4. Dead—
Fiction. 5. Interpersonal relations—Fiction. 6. Seashore—Fiction.] I. Title.
PZ7.S6807 Sw 2008   2008020220
[Fic]—dc22   CIP
                                                                          AC

Typography by Michelle Gengaro
1 2 3 4 5 6 7 8 9 10
❖

First Edition

For Lucy & Philip

Special thanks go to Stephanie Kip Rostan for finding the perfect editor for this book, to Farrin Jacobs for being the perfect editor for this book, and to everyone at HarperCollins for their hard work and enthusiasm.

To the staff of the Levine Greenberg Literary Agency: Thank you for taking care of the details so I don't have to. And to Monika Verma: I'm so lucky to have you as "my people." I am, as always, grateful for my early readers' comments, my family's support, and Sue Raffman's New York City apartment. Finally, thanks and love to Andrew Todhunter—I couldn't do it without you.

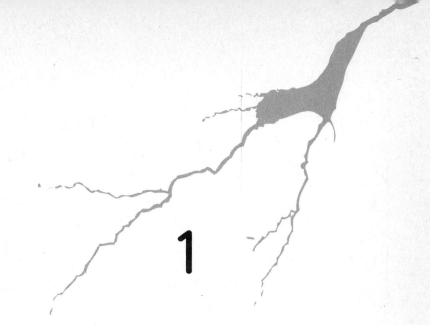

1

YOU'VE BEEN TO MY TOWN, or you've been to one just like it. You drove in on a sunny day in July, your father at the wheel of the minivan, your mother in the passenger seat, passing back juice boxes (which you'd outgrown years ago) while you pressed your nose to the window, searching for that first glimpse of blue water.

This is what you remember about my town: the wave that knocked you off your boogie board and dragged you along the ocean bottom. The ice cream—chocolate with fudge swirls—that you ate from an enormous homemade waffle cone. A tray of french fries seasoned with sand.

You remember the night you walked on the beach, the sand strangely cold on your sunburned feet, and stared up at the stars that shone so much brighter than they did at home.

Maybe you remember a storm, one more violent than any you'd ever seen before, the lightning so harsh and bright, it made your bare arms turn ghostly white. Then there was the thunder, coming one-Mississippi, two-Mississippi after the flashes, booming so hard that it shook the walls of your little rented cottage with the sand dune paintings on the walls. You started to cry, and your mother came to your bed and sang: *Hush, little baby, don't say a word. Mama's gonna buy you a mockingbird . . .*

Your mother's breathy voice made you stop crying, even though you were far too old for lullabies.

Then again, maybe you don't remember the thunderstorm. Or your mother's cornflower blue nightgown. Or the way she smelled like moisturizer and salt. Maybe you don't even remember the lullaby.

Because maybe you weren't really there on the night of the thunderstorm, in that little rented cottage with the sand dune paintings on the walls.

Maybe I was there instead.

2

DON'T FREAK OUT: It probably *wasn't* you I woke up in on that stormy night last July. Well, unless you're about five foot four, with pretty brown eyes and long, dark hair. Then it might have been you. (You might want to rethink that white-blond streak in your hair, by the way. It makes you look like a skunk.)

Note that I said that I "woke up" in your body (or, you know—somebody else's body). I didn't jump in or sneak in or steal in. I am not a body snatcher or a ghoul. I am a body switcher, which is totally different. I don't take over other people's bodies on purpose. And I always give them back.

So don't picture me as some bizarro Goth girl with dyed black hair, black lipstick, and a pierced eyebrow. I don't even own any black clothes. I am just a normal fifteen-year-old kid with normal fifteen-year-old problems: an overworked mother, a missing father. I worry about the usual stuff. Like, will a boy ever admire me for anything other than my killer butterfly stroke? And will I survive the first day of tenth grade without saying something stupid or losing my schedule or getting detention because I forgot to turn off my cell phone?

This is me: Claire Martin, fifteen years, five months old. I'm a Pisces, the sign of the fish, which is totally appropriate since I'm in the water about as much as a person can be without growing gills. My birthday is March 9–10; my birth certificate says March 10, but I was born on the stroke of midnight, so I think it should count as two days. My hair is brown, straight, shoulder length, and utterly resistant to anything resembling "a style." Mostly, I just pull my hair back with a plain elastic when it's still wet. My eyes are okay: hazel bordering on green but never quite getting there. I am five feet, seven inches tall. I will not tell you my weight because it is a big number, though I'm really just "solid," with virtually no body fat, even in places where it would be nice to have some. My best feature? My powerful shoulders. My worst feature? Ditto.

So, as you can see, aside from the occasional body switching (I mean, *really* occasional—a few times a year, tops), I am a completely normal, average, boring kid.

Okay, unless you factor in all of those conversations with my dead grandmother.

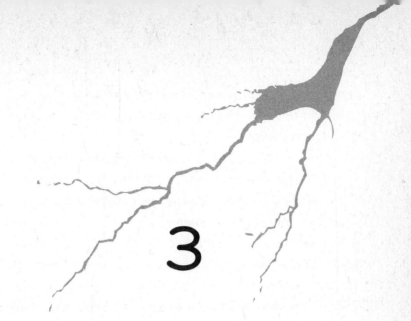

3

WHEN I WAS LITTLE, I thought I had a guardian angel. But then, who didn't? As far as I knew, everyone's guardian angel lounged at the end of her twin bed, smoking a ghostly cigarette and saying, "Your mother should really do something with her hair—all that gray and no style at all. No wonder she's never been married."

"She doesn't need a husband," I'd squeak, parroting what my mother had said a hundred times. "She's got a good job, and she's got me, and that's all she needs."

My angel would laugh her husky smoker's laugh and roll her eyes.

"You shouldn't smoke," I told my angel once. "It's bad for your health."

My angel took a long drag on her cigarette. She'd been smoking the same one for as long as I could remember, but it never got any smaller. She pursed her lips as if she were going to whistle and blew out a smoke ring, which floated up and hovered over her head like a halo.

"It's a little late for that, don't you think?"

"How did my grandmother die?" is my mother's second-least-favorite question. But she'll answer it—at least sort of—if I also ask her first-least-favorite question.

"Who was my father?" I'll never look her in the eyes when I ask this. I'll say it casually when I'm getting milk out of the fridge or staring out the car window.

"I'll tell you when you're older." She'll say this quickly, trying to move beyond the moment as fast as possible.

"You've been saying that for years. I'm older."

"Not old enough."

"Okay, then—what happened to my grandmother?" This time, I'll look at her. She won't look back.

Here she'll pause, consider. She can't refuse me twice. "She got sick and died. I was four years old."

"How did she die?"

"She died in the hospital."

"I didn't ask *where*, I asked *how*."

She'll bite her lip, look at her hands. "She got sick."

My angel wasn't much better—even once I realized who she was. I was six when I found out. My mother was looking for something in her desk, and she pulled out some loose photographs.

"It's the lady!" I squealed when I saw the black-and-white snapshot of Evelyn. She was wearing a long coat and a big hat, standing next to a car.

"What lady?" my mother asked, snatching up the photograph and shoving it back in her desk.

"The lady who sits on my bed. The lady who talks to me. My angel."

My mother turned white and said she needed some time alone. I went upstairs to my room and asked Evelyn why she'd never told me that she was my grandmother. She took an especially long drag on her infinite cigarette. And then a second. And a third. "I didn't want to get you in trouble," she said finally.

Sure enough, my mother took me to a shrink the very next week. We drew pictures and played games. It was fun. I didn't even know Dr. Bob was a shrink until Evelyn told me. She told me what to say, and I said it. There wasn't really a lady at the end of my bed. I just made that up. And all those times my mother heard me talking in my room? I had some imaginary friends. But I knew they weren't real—I mean, *duh*! After two visits, Dr. Bob diagnosed me as "creative" and "imaginative" and assured my mother she had nothing to worry about.

When I came home, I asked my angel what my mother and Dr. Bob had meant by "a family history of mental illness."

Here's what I know: My grandmother's name was Evelyn O'Shea—Evelyn Martin once she married my grandfather. She was six feet tall, with red hair that she wore in a heavy braid down her back. Her eyes were the color of the fog that rolls in from the ocean every afternoon.

Evelyn was tone deaf, but she loved to sing. She made bird calls. She talked to blue jays, but she was never crazy enough to

7

imagine that they understood her. She ate black licorice so much that her teeth were often gray. She spent hours combing the beach for sand dollars, which she insisted brought good luck. She loved to eavesdrop and gossip. She could sit on the beach for hours (with a hat and umbrella—her fair skin burned easily) just to watch the world walk by.

My grandfather, Charles, with a parade of housekeepers, raised my mother. He was Sandyland's first Dr. Martin. My mother, Lydia, is the second. On clear days, my grandfather would walk to his little office just off Main Street. He dropped dead of a heart attack two years before I was born. Whenever my mother talks about him, her eyes get glassy with tears. "I wish you'd met him. I wish he'd been able to see you, at least."

My mother works with two other family doctors in a health clinic near the highway. We live in the same house she grew up in, two blocks from the ocean, but she has to drive to work. She says we are lucky to live in our drafty blue bungalow, with its two small bedrooms and a bathroom upstairs. The upstairs was an addition, and it looks like it, as if someone just plopped a blue box onto the house. There is a pretty front porch that my mother had built with some of the money she inherited when her father died. My mother says, "We could never afford this house if we had to buy it now." The houses on either side of us belong to summer people, and their additions are larger and prettier. As my mother says, "Only people who don't live here can afford to live here."

My childhood was pretty nice, actually: three generations of Martin women living together in a cottage by the sea. So what if one of us was dead? Evelyn was my little secret, my cozy companion, the thing that made me special.

It never occurred to me to wonder why I was the only one who could see her.

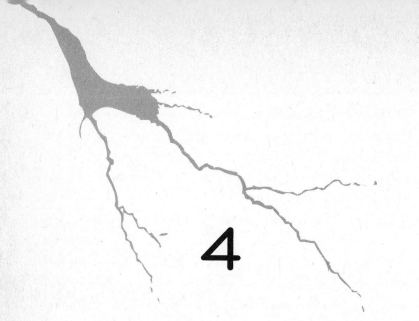

4

MY MOTHER SAYS I WAS AN EASY BABY. She hired a local woman to take care of me while she worked. The woman would leave me in my crib for hours while she watched talk shows and soap operas in the next room. If I cried, the woman would pick me up, but I hardly ever cried. Why would I? There was a beautiful red-haired woman standing over me, telling stories and singing songs in her off-key voice. She elicited my first smile, heard my first laugh.

Things chugged along pretty smoothly until the year I turned thirteen. I thought that might be significant—unlucky thirteen, and all that.

"There is nothing unlucky about the number thirteen," Evelyn told me, braiding her long, red hair. "It is just another number."

"Why now, then?" I asked.

"You're becoming a woman," she told me. "The party's over."

My first switch happened two years ago, on a sunny day in June. We were in seventh-grade science class with Mr. Peiteroski. Mr. P was a hands-on learning kind of guy: ocean drops under the microscope, beakers of clear stuff that turned fizzy when added to another beaker—that sort of thing.

Mr. Peiteroski was so jazzed about learning that he could barely sit still. He tended to spit when he talked. No one wanted to sit in the front row of his classroom. He had greasy black hair and the kind of oversize tortoiseshell glasses that were totally hip about twenty years ago. He wore wide ties and striped shirts that made him look even skinnier than he was. You'd think we'd all hate Mr. P and make fun of him mercilessly. The weird thing was, we all liked him. You could just tell he was a good person. Besides, he brought in donuts every Friday, and there's not a kid alive who can't be bribed with something fried and glazed.

It was the last week of school, and we were learning about electricity. I remember Mr. P saying something about grounding, and how during a thunderstorm you should avoid the highest ground, and how electricity always travels along the easiest path, as if it were something cunning and alive.

I wish I had paid more attention—it might have helped me understand what came later—but I was too busy counting down the time until school would be out for the summer and I could spend my days in icy waves instead of stuffy classrooms.

We were going to do an experiment, Mr. Peiteroski told us, his voice crackling with excitement. He had us all sit in a circle and hold hands. Our chairs screeched as we dragged them into the center of the room. On one side, I was stuck holding hands with this doughy, dopey kid. His name was Brandon, but everyone called him Pillsbury. He had sweaty hands. I couldn't wait for the experiment to be over.

A girl named Beanie was directly across from me. Beanie and I would become best friends, but I didn't know that yet. Back then my best friend was this girl called Avon, but she was in a different science class.

After making sure that we were all holding hands, Mr. P skittered over with a little wooden box with a switch on one side and different-colored wires sticking out of the top. Mr. P took one kid by the hand and then put his other hand on the box. "As soon as I flip this switch, I will take Marina's hand, which will make an unbroken chain! Remember, electricity always takes the easiest path!"

A few kids looked nervous. I wasn't scared. Mr. P would never hurt anyone.

He flipped the switch, and one girl yelped. The boy next to her giggled. Mr. P took the hand of the kid on his other side, creating a closed circle. The electricity traveled down the line, clicking through wrists, shooting through fingers.

It all happened so fast.

When the current reached me, I didn't yelp. I didn't giggle. I didn't say anything at all—because the force didn't simply pass through me with a pinch in one wrist and then the other. For a flash, I felt like I was floating near the ceiling, looking down at the classroom, the way they say you do when you die.

Then the current reached Beanie, and I wasn't watching from

above anymore. I was watching from the other side of the circle. I was staring at myself. I was staring back.

The current went around another time, and I blinked. I was back where I should be, next to Pillsbury. Beanie looked at me a little funny; I looked at her a little funny too. We said nothing.

I tried to forget about it. Just a little too much electricity. A dizzy spell. Water conducts electricity; everybody knows that. And Pillsbury's hands were so sweaty, they were practically dripping.

When I got home, Evelyn was in the kitchen, sitting at my mother's computer. Because she emits such a strong electrical force, she can make it work without even touching the keys; she just waves her hand over the keyboard and concentrates really hard. Evelyn says that MySpace has given her a whole new lease on life, which is quite an endorsement when you consider that Evelyn is actually dead.

"How was school?" she asked, as she did every day, logging off the computer. Since she died when my mother was four, Evelyn never got to do the welcome-home-from-school routine in real life, so she's trying to make up for it. Besides, it's not like she's got someplace better to be. As soon as she walks out the door, she gets lost in a fog.

Without looking at her, I opened the fridge and shrugged. My orange-and-white cat, Fluffernutter, ran into the room and began twining himself around my legs. Fluff can't see Evelyn. Or, if he can, he knows she can't feed him or let him outside, so he chooses to ignore her.

I pulled a can of cat food and a jug of milk out of the fridge.

Evelyn would get me an after-school snack if she could—which is to say, if she had a body.

"Is something wrong?" she asked, alarmed. "Did something happen?"

"Nothing's wrong," I said a little too sharply. "I've just got a lot of homework, is all." It didn't even occur to me to tell her what had happened. It never crossed my mind that she'd understand.

She frowned and checked my face. Then her expression softened with relief. "Hormones." She tapped her nose.

"What?"

"You've got a little pimple, sweetie. Right on the end of your nose. It's the hormones. They can affect your mood, too."

If only it were that simple.

5

EVELYN ASSURES ME I AM NOT A WITCH. She assured me of that three weeks later, after I ended up in a strange cottage, in a body I did not know.

Thunderstorms had never scared me. I'd lived my whole life in Sandyland, after all. We have no video arcades here, no miniature golf, no mall. But we have noisy, flashy storms, and you take your thrills where you can get them.

It was the first big storm of the summer, and I was sitting up in bed, admiring the way the lightning lit the old maple tree in our yard like the beam from a lighthouse. I remember the storm coming closer: five-Mississippi, then four-Mississipi, then three. I hoped it would pass over my house with a giant flash-boom, an electrical explosion, an adrenaline rush.

It never made it to my house; or, if it did, I had already gone. At two-Mississippi, I was flooded with heat, like when you stand too close to a bonfire and the wood suddenly tumbles down, releasing an eruption of sparks. The lightning flashed, and it was like I became part of the light, the power, the surge.

I blacked out, only for a few minutes, I think, though it may have been longer.

I woke up in a room I had never seen before, the storm still raging outside. I leaped out of bed and came face-to-face with a mirror—but the brown eyes staring back at me were not my own.

I screamed. There was a shuffling sound in the hallway, and a woman came in, her eyebrows arched with concern, her light eyes wide with love.

"Kimmy, baby, are you okay?"

I shook my head no, my throat too tight with fear to speak. I kept staring at the mirror. Every time the lightning flashed, I'd get a quick, overlit view of the girl's face, like a camera bulb going off over and over.

Kimmy's mother took me in her soft arms. Her hair was black, like her daughter's, only without the thick white streak. She smelled like the yellow moisturizer you put on after you've been in the sun all day. I clutched her, sobbing wildly, the wailing sound unfamiliar to me, so much higher and squeakier than my own cries.

"It's just a thunderstorm," Kimmy's mother cooed. "You haven't been scared of thunder since you were a little girl."

I buried my head in her shoulder and nodded as if I believed her. She led me back to the bed, which was narrow, hard, and covered with a nubby white bedspread. I lay down, quivering as she sang the mockingbird song over and over. I squeezed my eyes shut. Maybe if I didn't see this unfamiliar woman, this unfamiliar room, they would stop being real. Kimmy's mother sang until I finally drifted off into a dreamless sleep.

When I woke up the next morning, I was back in my own bed, Evelyn lounging at the end with her usual cigarette. "It's time we had a talk," she said.

Evelyn told me the universe is filled with electrical fields none of us can see—invisible highways and paths that swerve and veer and join us in ways most people would never imagine. According to Evelyn, she and I have unusually strong electrical and magnetic fields that jump and pull against our will. Normally, the pulls are not strong enough to take us out of our bodies. The danger comes when the electrical forces around us become so powerful that the electricity within us darts out to join them. When that happens, our spirits look for a body to land in, much the same way that lightning seeks the quickest path to the ground.

That's when we switch.

"Can I land in *any* body?" I asked, my eyes widening at the thought of looking into a mirror and seeing Pillsbury or Mr. P staring back at me.

She shook her head. "When you were born, the moon set your magnetic signature. You can only switch with a close match, someone who was born under the same moon as you." I checked the moon cycles for the year I was born: I can switch with someone born a week before or three weeks after me. Because males and females emit different magnetic fields, I only switch with girls.

"How do you know all of this?" I asked Evelyn once the shock

17

of what she had told me had sort of sunk in. "Did someone tell you? Someone from . . . beyond?"

She looked up at the ceiling. "No one told me anything. I just figured it out."

I stared at her. "So, do you *know* this? Or are you just making it up?"

She scowled at me and pulled herself up tall. "You got a better explanation?"

So far, Evelyn has been right. I only switch with girls my own age who have birthdays in March. I only switch during an electrical "event"—a thunderstorm, usually. Afterward, when the outside forces dissipate, and I fall asleep, I return to my own body.

Now, when a storm approaches, I close my eyes and breathe deeply. Switching doesn't hurt, really. I just can't breathe for a moment, like when you get the wind knocked out of you. When I arrive—wherever I arrive—I keep my eyes closed for a few moments and take a deep breath. Sometimes I try to guess where I've landed, though in the summer it's almost impossible because there are so many strangers around.

Storms tend to hit Sandyland at night, which works well. I don't mind sleeping in strange beds, at least not too much. One time I ended up in a tent off the beach. That was a rough night, and I barely slept, but the next morning, as always, I wound up back in my own bed, my body feeling oddly relaxed and refreshed. One stormy day I switched during the afternoon and found myself in a roomful of people watching a slasher movie on DVD. The family all looked so bored with one another and so annoyed to be stuck missing a beach day because of the rain that nobody said a

18

thing, but just stared and stared at the little television set. I leaned back into the scratchy couch (which smelled of mildew) and closed my eyes. When I opened them again, I was home.

And what of my own body? What happens when someone else looks in the mirror and sees me looking back?

"I won't let that happen," Evelyn said softly. "Whenever you leave your body, I'll jump in and hold your place." Finally she looked me in the eye. "What happened to me . . . I won't let it happen to you."

"What happened to you?" I asked, unsure whether I really wanted to hear the answer.

"You are a gift to me," she said, ignoring the question. "Before you were born, I felt myself fading away. It was like I was looking at your mother and grandfather through a dense fog. Your birth let me see again."

If I am a gift to Evelyn, her gift to me is this: Whenever she sees my spirit leaving my body, she jumps in it to hold my place.

We weren't sure if it would work, at first. Evelyn wasn't born under the same moon as I. Heck, when I was born, she wasn't even *alive*. But she's been floating around for so long and has absorbed so much random energy that she's become a kind of universal donor of switching.

"Think of it as musical chairs," she told me. "We've got three spirits and two bodies. If your body is suddenly vacant and I'm right there, I should be able to slip in first."

I thought of a hotel with a "Vacancy" sign one minute, a "No Vacancy" the next. I liked the chair idea better. But however you

19

want to look at it, Evelyn was right: As long as she's nearby, she can switch into my body the instant I leave it.

As for the third spirit, the one without a chair (which sounds much better than "without a body"), it's left to hover in a kind of unconscious in-between state that resembles neither life nor death. Evelyn says I should think of it as a kind of deep, peaceful sleep. I try to.

The next (and last) time I switched with the girl named Kimmy, I snuck into the yard to see where her rented cottage was: a block from my own house, closer to the ocean. I sniffed the sea air and then tiptoed back inside, slipping under Kimmy's nubby white bedspread.

In the morning I awoke in my own bed, with a stomachache.

"It worked!" Evelyn crowed from the end of my bed. While I'd been tiptoeing around Kimmy's cottage, Evelyn had been raiding the freezer. She'd been craving ice cream for forty years. It was just as good as she remembered, though maybe she should have passed on that third bowl.

Now I'm no longer shocked when I look in the mirror and see someone else's face peering back. I tell myself that it's not so bad, that it will only happen when lightning gets too close, and mostly in the summer, when Sandyland's population doubles. I tell myself that ultimately I'm in control: To return to my body, all I have to do is sleep.

I told myself all of this for two years. And I believed myself. That was my mistake.

6

THE FIRST TIME I SAW THE GIRL, I was walking along the beach with Beanie. We had left the wide public stretch and were strolling along a narrow strip of sand that disappeared at high tide. A wall of boulders parallel to the beach kept the ocean from washing away the expensive houses that rose above it. Each house had a set of concrete steps leading to the beach. Each set of steps had a sign that read, PRIVATE PROPERTY: KEEP OFF STEPS. Other signs told us to KEEP OFF ROCKS. Walking on the beach was allowed, if reluctantly.

We went all the way to the water's edge, the chilly sea licking our feet. An occasional seashell glinted through the froth before slipping back into the surf.

Beanie and I wore our red lifeguard swimsuits—hers a one piece, mine a two, both with racing backs. It was the last day of sea-guard camp, and my muscles felt floppy from a morning spent battling the waves, paddling on a surfboard, and hauling a succession

21

of fake drowners back to the shore. It was my fifth summer in the camp. I'd passed my certification test long ago, and there wasn't much more for me to learn, but I liked the routine of running into the ocean on foggy mornings. Besides, my mother worked long hours at the health clinic, and I liked having someplace to go.

Next year I'd be sixteen, which meant I could get a job as a junior guard, helping teach some of the younger kids about water safety. Until then, I had to make do with the money I earned from babysitting. Thanks to my mother's endless referrals, I was booked practically every Saturday night. Not all of the kids were as well behaved as my mother made them out to be, but she spared me the biters and the bed wetters, at least.

The girl was sitting on a towel in front of what Beanie and I called the Ice Cube House. It was all gray concrete and tinted glass, boxy and ugly in a big-money kind of way. Next to the girl, two little blond boys, dressed in identical orange swim trunks, dug in the sand.

The girl was wearing one of those three-triangle bikinis: two tiny triangles on top, one slightly larger one on the bottom. The suit was chocolate brown with silver and turquoise beads on the straps. I tried to imagine swimming in something like that. One good wave, and that bathing suit would be on its way to South America.

She leaned back on her elbows, legs together, pretty knees bent in front of her. Her toenails were painted hot pink. A fly buzzed around her slender feet. Her tummy was perfectly flat, her legs almost unnaturally long. Her blond hair was thick and streaky—probably out of a bottle.

Next to me, Beanie tugged at the bottom of her bathing suit, which had a habit of riding up. Like me, Beanie had spent the entire summer in the ocean. She'd hoped to lose some weight, to fit into smaller-size jeans, at least, but all she had to show for her effort was an extra inch or two around her shoulders. Beanie's mother says she should have gone to fat camp, like last year. Beanie's mother has big, big hair. I think she wears it that way to hide her horns.

As for me, my mother says I have a "beautiful, strong body." It's strong, all right, and not fat at all—but beautiful? Not really. Sturdy is more like it. My shoulders are too wide, my bust too small. I have a flat butt and virtually no waist. Mine is the ideal V-shaped swimmer's body, which is totally hot—if you're a guy.

Beanie and I smiled at the girl and said hi—because that's what you do in Sandyland when you pass someone on the beach. Her eyes flickered toward us and then out to sea while the little boys continued to play at her feet. She said nothing.

Beanie and I continued along the beach. We were quiet for a short while, feeling weirdly hurt. Then I said, "She didn't mean to be rude. She's just upset because she lost her tiara in the sand."

Beanie hooted. Beanie has one of those laughs, loud and musical, that makes everyone around her laugh even harder. "Or maybe she's lonely," she whooped. "Maybe Ken stood her up."

"Maybe Ken ran off with one of the Bratz dolls," I said. "Maybe Ken likes the babes with the big heads."

We laughed until our stomachs hurt.

I am not a total tomboy. When I was little, I had Barbies just like everybody else. My Barbies' hair was always ratty, though, because I used to take them into the bathtub and pretend they were racing in an Olympic-size pool. Also, I bent all their knees the wrong way—just to see what would happen. After that, they didn't kick very well.

Beanie and I walked until we ran out of beach, the surf slamming into the rock wall. We turned around and headed back, staring at the massive houses rather than the ocean. "I'll take one of those," I said, pointing to a gray shingled house with a copper chimney shaped like a lighthouse.

"I'll buy the one next to you, then," Beanie said, gesturing toward a brown A-frame. The blinds were all shut. Most of these houses were barely even used.

When we passed the Ice Cube House on the way back, we were disappointed to see that the girl had left the beach. We were all set to say, "Hey! How are you? Are you just visiting, or is this your house?" and pretty much just keep talking until she was forced to acknowledge our existence. But she had moved up to the lawn. She lay on a lounge chair, eyes closed, facing the sun, while the little boys scampered around her, tossing fistfuls of goldfish crackers at each other.

"Babysitting for rich people," I muttered. "Nice summer job."

"Yeah, really," Beanie said.

By the time we reached the public beach, we'd forgotten all about her.

Beanie and I have known each other since we were five years old. We had no choice, really. There's only one elementary school in town, with one class per grade, so everybody knows everybody, often better than we'd like. Until last year, we were never really friends, though. Beanie was always nice to me, but I didn't think much of it because she was always nice to everybody. Back then, if I'd had to think of one word to describe Beanie, that word would've been *jolly*, and I didn't do jolly. Then there was her name, which seemed so goofy. I mean—Beanie? It made me think of jelly beans and beanbag animals and stupid little hats. Beanie's real name is Bernice, so you can't exactly blame her for going with a nickname. I just thought she could have come up with something a little more dignified.

Up until eighth grade I was best friends with Avon (which, for some reason, I didn't think was a stupid name). Avon and I were nothing alike. She was all about manicures and movie stars, while I loved swimming and animals. But Avon and I were born two hours apart—in the same hospital, no less—so our friendship seemed inevitable. Beanie was born only ten days later, but until a couple of years ago her birthday seemed insignificant.

The next time we saw the girl was a few days later. Even though sea-guard camp was over, Beanie and I were at the beach because there was no place else to go, and besides, we never got sick of the beach no matter how much time we spent there. Beanie and I wore our regular bathing suits instead of the red guard ones. Mine was a blue-and-purple tie-dyed tank with a racer back. Beanie wore board shorts over her one-piece because she hates her thighs.

We were sitting in front of the lifeguard stand. There was no lifeguard down by the rocks; the rich people just had to know how to swim. In front of us, out a way, a yellow swim float bobbed in the waves. It was covered with seagulls, which meant that later, when all of us kids swam out to it, it would be covered with bird crap.

The girl was at the beach, but I didn't see her at first. All I saw was Nate Jameson.

"Nate alert," I whispered to Beanie, who was sitting on a towel next to me, rubbing suntan lotion onto her arms.

"Where?"

"Snack shack."

We gazed out to sea for a long moment. Beanie closed her lotion with a snap and dropped the bottle in the sand.

"I could really go for some onion rings right about now," she said. "You?"

I pretended to think about it. "It's a little early for onion rings. But maybe a shake."

We stood up, brushed the sand off our legs, and sauntered over to the parking lot. Nate stood to the side of the snack shack, waiting for an order. The snack shack is white wood and boxy, with bright blue trim. It's been here since before I was born, and the grease they use to cook the fries and onion rings may well be older than me. Not that I'd let that stop me. Food safety is for wimps.

Beanie and I pretended to be deep in conversation. Actually, we *were* deep in conversation:

Me: Does my hair look all right?
Beanie: Your hair looks cute.

Me: I shouldn't have gone swimming. My hair would look better if I hadn't gone swimming.

Beanie: Nate has seen you with swim-hair a million times. A billion times.

Me: Maybe that's the problem. Maybe if Nate saw me with dry hair, he'd think of me in a whole new way.

I was out of my league with Nate. I knew that. Nate was a year older than me. He'd been the junior lifeguard in my camp group—what you'd call a junior counselor if the camp were on land. Next week he'd be starting eleventh grade at Sandyland High.

Nate was the strongest swimmer in the guard program. He was the best freestyler on the high-school swim team. And he was the most drop-dead gorgeous creature I'd ever seen, with blond curls that got lighter and curlier as the summer went on, green eyes that went from wide to crinkly when he smiled, and a nose that would be absolutely straight if not for a fight he'd gotten into with Ryan Kenner in the fourth grade.

None of that would matter if Nate weren't so perfectly good, so perfectly nice. He noticed when I refined my butterfly stroke. He cheered as I hauled Beanie—in her dramatic role as a drowning tourist—out of the surf. ("I lost my diamonds in the waves!" she'd shrieked. "We must go back for my diamonds!") He gave me advice about sophomore teachers: which ones gave the most homework, which ones could be convinced to talk about themselves for the entire class when they should have been teaching algebra.

27

Nate liked me: I knew that. He liked me—and here we approach the most dreaded phrase in the English language—as a friend.

As we got closer to the snack shack, I noticed that Ryan Kenner was behind the counter. Ryan had reigned in his aggressive impulses since breaking Nate's nose (rumor has it he went to counseling), but he was still a nasty dweeb who was too tall and too skinny, with a sharp nose and a perpetual meanish grin. He had shaggy reddish-blondish hair and skin that didn't tan. Mostly, he looked right through me, which was just fine. Beanie said I was too hard on him. She liked Ryan, even though she recognized that it might be because she associated Ryan with fried food and she really, really loved fried food.

Behind Ryan, Alexei was working the grill. Alexei had come over on a special summer work permit from Russia or one of those other Russian-ish countries. He had yellowish hair and a red face—but probably anyone who spent all of his days alternating between a grill and a fryer would be flushed. He was short but powerful. I say I'm strong, but trust me: Alexei could snap me in two. He wouldn't, though. He's completely and totally kind, and not just because he lacks the vocabulary to be rotten. When he says, "Is nice day, yah? Is sunny, yah?" you just know he's being sincere.

Beanie is in love with Alexei, which kind of makes sense and kind of doesn't. It make sense because he's so sweet and kind of cute, but it doesn't because Beanie is so witty and charming, most of which is lost on Alexei and his fifty-word vocabulary.

According to Beanie, that's the whole point: "It takes the

pressure off, you know? I never have to worry about being funny, about saying the right thing. I can say, 'Hey, Lex, is it hot back there?' every time—and every time, he'll laugh and smile because he's just so happy to understand me."

Anyway, Beanie and I stood a few feet away from the counter, squinting at the giant, hand-painted menu posted over the order window. This was for effect. We knew exactly what was on the menu, which had been the same for as long as we could remember: hamburgers, hot dogs, fried clams, breakfast burritos, fish-and-chips, milk shakes, fries. And onion rings, of course.

"Hey," Nate called out. I looked over, wide-eyed with fake surprise, and blinked a few times, finally allowing my face to register recognition. He was wearing faded, navy blue swim trunks that hung low on his waist, a slightly damp white T-shirt that was tight at his shoulders and loose around his stomach, and a shell necklace. His feet were bare and sandy.

He sauntered over, grinning. He reached out his arm and made a fist. "Dude," he said.

"Dude," I responded, holding up my fist and tapping his knuckles. A chill ran down my arm.

Beanie and I have discussed Nate's whole "dude" thing. I like it, but it does kind of seem, well, guy-ish. Beanie insists it's a gender-neutral term and a sign of affection.

"Catch any waves today?" I asked.

Nate laughed and ran a hand through his damp blond curls. "Oh, yeah—major crush." This is a running joke between us. (Beanie says that running jokes are another sign of a deep and potentially lasting affection.) Sandyland bills itself as the

29

"World's Safest Beach," but it could just as easily advertise itself as the "World's Crappiest Surf Spot." I know how to surf—most of us do—but there are only a few days every summer when the waves are big enough to justify taking out the board.

The sunlight caught Nate's green eyes, making them almost luminescent. "You're going out for the swim team again, aren't you?" he asked. "Time trials are the second day of school."

"Well, yeah," I said. "Though I've spent so much time ocean swimming, I'm kind of out of practice on my strokes."

"You'll do great," Nate said. "Your butterfly's just amazing."

And then his expression changed, softened. His eyes widened. His smile faded—not from disappointment but with something that looked like awe. For an instant, I thought it was because of me, because of my flawless butterfly stroke. Maybe I was like a butterfly myself, just crawling out of my chrysalis, newly transformed.

My entire body grew warm. The world was suddenly more beautiful, more golden. It was like the last moment of a glorious dream, when you believe—honestly know—that you can fly. Or that you've won a gold medal in the Olympics. Or that you know your father's name.

And then you wake up and you realize it was all just a dream, and all you want to do is cry.

That's how it felt when I realized Nate wasn't looking at me at all. He was looking behind me.

She was wearing the brown bathing suit again, the one with all the strings and beads. There were even beads between the two tiny triangles that (barely) covered her breasts. She had a towel tied around her waist, so at least we were spared a view of her butt cheeks.

I hadn't gotten a good look at her face before. Now I saw that she was even exquisite from the neck up, with bee-stung lips, a tiny nose, and arched eyebrows. Her eyes were nothing special—smallish, brownish—but it hardly mattered. Her hair was a streaky blond, thick and wild.

I hated her. I hated her more than I'd ever hated anyone, even Avon.

She had the little boys with her again. "I want an ice-cream sundae!" one whined.

"They don't have sundaes, Cameron," she answered in a flat, nasal voice, her eyes fixed on the menu over the counter.

"I wanna sundae!" The way he said it, *sundae* had about five syllables: "sun-dae-ae-ae-ae."

She rolled her eyes. "You can have a shake. Prescott, you want a shake too?"

"Fries!" Prescott commanded. He was half a head shorter than his brother, but his voice was just as loud.

She approached the counter and tucked her wild blond hair behind her ears. Ryan smiled at her as she ordered. She didn't smile back.

"Anything for yourself?" Ryan asked, all bug-eyed and drooling. What did he expect her to answer—"A dream date with you"?

She shrugged her bony shoulders. "Just give me a diet soda."

Beanie and I exchanged glances: We could have called that one.

Ryan shouted the order to Alexei, who, to his credit, only stared for a second or five before turning back to his baskets. The girl shuffled off to the side to wait for her order, her arms crossed over her midriff as if in modesty. Sure, I thought: Give the world a good look at your boobs, but cover your tummy.

Beanie, ready to order, stepped up to the counter. "Hi, Ryan."

"Huh?" He was still watching the girl. Then: "Oh, hi." Nate was watching the girl too, I noticed, though not so obviously. My face burned.

"How are the onion rings today?" Beanie asked Ryan, her glaze flickering beyond him to Alexei.

Ryan's eyes shot over to the girl, then back at Beanie. He looked annoyed at the distraction. "You should know," he said, his stupid grin finally gone. "You eat more onion rings than everyone else put together."

You'd think the moment would be silent, that the whole world would stop talking, but this was the beach, and the beach is always noisy. The little blond boys yelped at each other, the waves roared, kids on the beach yelled and laughed. Nate was silent, but that was just because he was so mesmerized by the girl, who was frowning at the menu, not noticing him at all.

Alexei looked up from the fryer. He stared at Ryan and then at Beanie before giving his attention back to a basket of french fries. It wasn't clear whether he'd heard Ryan or if he understood him. I felt like I should say something to Ryan, come to Beanie's defense, but I know Beanie, and she just wanted this moment to be over.

"Okay, I'll just have some, then," she muttered. "A small."

I ordered my shake, and we sat down at the lone picnic table to wait. The table was covered with crumbs and a few abandoned burrito wrappers. Beanie crossed her arms in front of herself and blinked a couple of times, trying not to cry. Her pretty blue eyes turned pink around the edges.

"He's an ass," I mouthed.

She nodded a little and bit her lip, like she didn't really believe me but wished she could.

When Nate's breakfast burrito came out, instead of taking it to the beach like he normally does, he came over to the table. "Hey, guys," he said.

"We're *girls*," I wanted to say to him. But instead I just said, "Hey, Nate," and tried to smile.

Rather than putting his food on the table, he sat facing out— toward the order window, toward the girl—and ate off of his lap. From the corner of my eye, I saw her towel slip down her hips. She yanked it back up and re-knotted the terry.

When Ryan called out her order, Nate dumped his burrito on the table and sprang over to the window. "Can I help you with that?" he asked as she reached for her cardboard tray.

"No," she said, barely looking at him.

"There's room at the table," Nate said. "If you want to sit."

She looked at him steadily for a moment and then—astonishingly—rolled her eyes and turned away.

"Cameron, Prescott—we're going," she said.

"I want my fries!"

She handed the fry bag to Prescott and the shake to his older brother. She tossed the cardboard tray in the trash and took a long drag on her diet soda. Then she walked away, the boys following, Prescott leaving a trail of french fries like a modern-day Hansel.

Nate just stood there, abandoned on the sandy asphalt, his eyes wide and sad as he watched her leave.

I knew just how he felt.

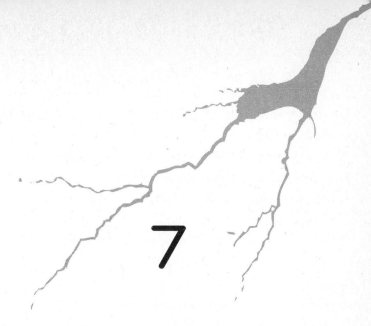

7

BEANIE THINKS WE TELL EACH OTHER EVERYTHING, and I wish that were true. Once she said, "Sometimes I feel like we're the same person," and I just stared at her until her smile fell and she said, "What?"

"Nothing," I said. "That's how I feel too."

But Beanie doesn't know about my body switching—and she certainly doesn't know that I've switched into hers. I'm afraid she'd think it was creepy. It is creepy.

Beanie's got enough body issues already; she doesn't need this. But every once in a while, she'll mention her "freaky dreams," in which she floats around my bedroom, looking down on me.

I'll say, "Oh, yeah—I've had that dream too!" And then, before she has too much time to think about the floating dream, I'll ask, "Have you ever dreamed that you got to school and there was a test that you didn't know about? Or that you got to school and realized you were still in your pajamas?"

And she'll say, "Yes!"

And I'll say, "Weird how everybody has the same kinds of dreams."

I wasn't completely surprised when I switched with Beanie for the second time. I'd been in her body once before, after all. I thought she might live too far away—just under a mile—but the storm that came that night was especially violent.

I'd been in Beanie's house once for a birthday party in elementary school, but I'd never been in her room. Beanie was so sunny, so giggly, that I would have expected a bedroom decorated in rainbow colors, or maybe pink and purple.

Her room was white. I mean, really, really white: white furniture, white bedspread, white rug, white walls. When the lightning flashed, it felt like I was in an overexposed picture.

I turned on the bedside lamp, which gave the room a soft yellow glow. There was no clutter: no earrings left on the dresser, no magazines on the nightstand, no trophies or piggy banks lining the shelves. Everything was stored in plastic bins, under the bed and in the closet. I peeked into the hallway and saw more white carpet, more white walls. The entire place smelled vaguely of bleach.

Let's just say it was not the kind of house where you would eat Cheetos in bed.

The only photos in Beanie's room were taped to her dresser mirror. I crept over to get a closer look, startling a bit when I saw Beanie's face staring back from the mirror just as a huge clap of thunder shook the room. The face in the mirror startled too. I smiled. Beanie's face smiled back.

This would never stop being weird.

The photographs on the mirror were all of Beanie, unsmiling, in a plain blue bathing suit. There she was, front, side, and back. A sheet of yellow notebook paper was taped under the photos. It listed days and weights, with smiley faces next to the lower numbers. I checked today's date: up a pound. Sad face.

There was a diary in Beanie's top dresser drawer, a thick book with worn corners. I knew it was wrong to read it, but I did anyway, opening to a random page.

> **June 10**—School was serving pizza today and it smelled so good but I just had diet cola and some carrots and celery from home. Stomach so empty in math class it made noises and everybody looked at me. Drank two bottles of water, which helped a little. Almost made it to dinner but I had those candy bars under my bed and it was like they were talking to me and after a while I couldn't think about anything else until I had one, couldn't do my homework, even. Ate three. Hate myself.
>
> What I ate today: Rice Krispies with skim milk, 9 baby carrots, 4 pieces celery, 3 Snickers (full size), skinless chicken breast, broccoli, lemon water
>
> **June 11**—1 grapefruit, Cheerios with skim milk, ½ tomato sandwich (on light bread), banana, hard-boiled egg, 2 tomato slices, 2 Milky Ways (full size)

June 12—Mom looked under my bed and found
the candy bars. She says it is my own fault I am so
fat. I started to cry and she said I am weak. I said
I was going for a run. I started to but then I went
to McDonald's instead.

What I ate today: Rice Krispies with skim
milk, apple, nonfat yogurt, bowl of iceberg
lettuce, Quarter Pounder with cheese, large
fries, large chocolate shake, apple pie.

June 13—Did experiment with electricity in science
class. Felt really weird and dizzy and like I left my
body. Like I was dead or something. I think it is
because I hadn't eaten anything all day but a
grapefruit and three crackers. Low blood sugar?

I closed the book and slid it back into its spot in Beanie's
drawer. My heart—Beanie's heart—was thudding. I looked in the
mirror, expecting to see someone fleshy and grotesque, but all I
saw was Beanie: sweet, friendly Beanie, her face a little round, her
edges a little soft, her brown hair curling daintily around her
cheeks. Her tiny nose was sprinkled with freckles. She had tears
in her blue eyes.

I switched with Beanie one other time that summer, during
a storm so wild it knocked out everyone's electricity. That
time, I was prepared. I loosened the tape around the yellow
weight chart until it peeled away from the mirror and dropped
it behind the dresser. I looked in the mirror, right at the spot
where the chart had been, and waited for the lightning to flash.

"You're beautiful," I told Beanie's soft face. "You have lovely blue eyes and a great smile and elegant long fingers."

And then I crawled between her rough white sheets and went to sleep.

I've been in Beanie's room lots of times since then, of course, but only in my own body. She still has a picture of herself wearing a bathing suit, but now the suit is red and the photo is framed. I'm standing next to her in a matching red tank, our arms around each other's powerful shoulders. We are laughing.

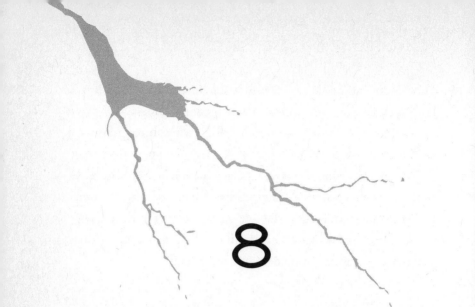

8

WHEN I WAS LITTLE, I thought we were rich. It wasn't that my mother drove a flashy car or wore nice clothes or took me on big vacations. She did none of that. It was because other kids would say, "Your mother is a doctor, so you must be rich." And: "You live close to the beach, so you must be rich."

Then one day I told my mother that Avon's family was going to Hawaii, and I thought it would be nice if we went too. Avon said the hotel's pool had a waterfall, a cave, and two waterslides. They were going to take a helicopter ride over a volcano. Avon's father is also a doctor, a plastic surgeon. He drives an hour and a half to his office, where he charges big bucks to make boobs bigger and noses smaller.

When I was little, Avon and I used to pretend we were sisters. That was my idea. She thought I came up with it because I liked her so much and because I was an only child. And that was part of it. Mostly, though, I figured, if Avon were my sister, then

Dr. Stanley would be my father. With his heavy workload and long commute, Dr. Stanley was never around much, and when he was home, he tended to watch TV or work on his computer. But to my mind, a distant father was better than no father at all.

At any rate, when I told my mother about the Stanleys' vacation, she smiled—sort of. "Hawaii would be nice."

"Why don't we go, then?"

"Honey, we can't afford it."

"But you're a doctor! We're rich!"

That was when she broke the news that family doctors don't make the kind of money that surgeons do and that the only reason we live so close to the water is that she inherited the house from her father. Later I learned that it was more than that. She lets a lot of her patients just pay what they can afford. Some of them don't pay at all. Others are on long-term, interest-free payment plans. "It's not right to profit from another person's suffering," she told me.

That seemed like a ridiculous thing for a doctor to say—like a mechanic saying it is wrong to profit from another person's leaky transmission or a barber saying it is wrong to profit from another person's hair growth.

"So are we . . . poor?" I asked her, worried.

"Of course not," she said. "I've got money saved for your college and for my retirement. We have everything we need and most of what we want." She took my hand and looked me in the eye. "We're very lucky."

I nodded as if I believed her, even as I thought, *Lucky people fly helicopters over volcanoes. Lucky people have fathers.*

Still, every year in late August, my mother and I act like lucky people. She takes a day off of work. She wears her nicest pair of slacks and even a little lipstick. (Since my mother wears a white coat over her clothes five days a week, she doesn't normally pay much attention to her clothes.) She wears her straight, shoulder-length hair down even though it parts like curtains around her ears. (*Evelyn is right*, I think disloyally. My mother's hair is getting too gray. She really should start coloring it.)

And then, the big event: We go to the mall.

The mall is nothing special. But since it is forty-five minutes away, it is the only place we ever go where my mother doesn't run into any of her patients. In Sandyland, we'll pop into the Rite Aid for a quick tube of toothpaste, and within three minutes some lady with a shopping cart full of mucus-covered kids will be screeching, "Dr. Martin! I was just going to call you about Terrence! I think he has pinkeye—it's all red and oozing, and now his sister's eye is starting to look a little funny. Terrence and Taylor, look at Dr. Martin—right at her, hold your chins up. See?"

"So, what are we looking for?" my mother asked as we strode across the open-air parking lot. It was a clear, blue-skied morning, warm but not humid. *A perfect beach day*, I thought. As much as I hated to think about it, school would be starting in two days.

"The usual," I said. "Sneakers, jeans." I thought of Nate standing next to the snack shack in his damp white T-shirt. "Maybe something nicer. Like, I don't know, a skirt or something."

My mother looked at me, startled. I hadn't worn a skirt—at least not willingly—since I was six years old. "Whatever you want," she said with forced casualness. "It's your day."

42

I looked stupid in skirts. That was obvious immediately.

"You don't look stupid in skirts," my mother said as we stared at my reflection in the dressing-room mirror. I'd tried on a short, pleated one, royal-blue-with-black plaid. "That skirt looks too much like a school uniform—it would look stupid on anyone. Try another style."

The other styles weren't any better. First I tried a turquoise peasant thing. "It makes me look stubby," I said.

My mother shook her head. "It's not you, it's the skirt."

It was the skirt again when I tried on a denim knee-length.

"Let's just get jeans." I sighed, feeling defeated. I knew just where to find jeans that would fit me: in the boys' department.

"How about we try some other stores after lunch?" my mother suggested.

I nodded. I wished I were in the ocean, my body completely submerged.

For lunch we bypassed the food court in favor of a chain restaurant, where we ordered gourmet pizzas: barbeque chicken for me, some gross thing with olives for my mother.

"So," she said as we sipped our ice water, waiting for our food to arrive. "Sophomore year. Wow."

"Mm." I pulled a sugar packet from the little plastic cube in the center of the table just to have something to fiddle with. I tipped it one way and then another, the grains of sugar sliding like sand in an hourglass.

"Are you excited?" my mother asked. "About a whole new set of classes?"

I shrugged.

"Maybe a little nervous?"

I considered. "No." Of course I was nervous, but talking about it would only make things worse.

At least it wouldn't be as bad as last year, when I didn't even know my way around the building. Going into ninth grade, I already knew a lot of people because Sandyland is one of those places where "everyone knows everyone." (I know that that sounds cozy, but trust me: It's mostly just annoying.) But Sandyland High is a regional school, which meant that there were even more people I didn't recognize. I couldn't believe how old some of the kids looked. They must have been held back, like, three or four years. There were guys with thick beards and girls with tattoos. There were a lot of pierced eyebrows.

My mother drank some water, the ice clinking in her glass. Her eyelids fluttered nervously. For two people who have lived together for fifteen years, my mother and I have never been great at conversation.

"Do you like the new carpet?" my mother asked. She'd just covered the worn wood floors upstairs with wall-to-wall.

"It's nice," I said. "It's fine." The carpet was beige polyester—how excited could I get? The house smelled vaguely of Scotchgard.

She put her water glass on the table and cleared her throat. "You know, in my practice, I sometimes see kids. From your school."

"Uh-huh." Was Nate one of her patients? No way was I going to ask. Beanie still went to the pediatrician she'd been seeing since she was born. She really liked him, but she said the *Highlights* magazines in the waiting room were getting kind of old.

I put the sugar packet back, pulled out a Sweet'N Low and tilted it to one side. Too powdery: it didn't have the same hour-glass effect.

My mother cleared her throat again. "Some of the kids, they—not all of them, I know it's not everyone, but some of the kids . . ." She took a deep breath and spread her fingers out on the table, as if for balance. "You're getting older, and sometimes things are different. Than they were before, I mean. And the pressure—sometimes a kid can feel pressured."

I looked up at her. Her face was bright red.

"I won't do drugs, Mom."

She nodded rapidly, her face still red. "I know. I mean, I never thought you would. But there's other, there are other . . . things. Temptations . . ."

"I won't drink, either. Or smoke. I promise." My mother had been lecturing me on the evils of alcohol since I was about six. I had never seen her drink anything stronger than iced tea.

But this wasn't about alcohol. Her eyebrows were raised. She was waiting for more. "What?" I asked.

She took a deep breath. "Chastity Dunhauser," she said finally. Chastity Dunhauser was an honor-roll student at Sandyland High until she got pregnant in the tenth grade (talk about ironic). Now she takes care of her baby during the day and works night shifts at the Rite Aid.

45

"You're afraid I'm going to work at Rite Aid?" I deadpanned. She laughed in spite of herself and threw her napkin at me. "No Rite Aid!" I said, laughing. "I swear!"

After lunch we went to a store that girls at school were always talking about. It was dark and the music was really loud. My mother flinched when we walked in but held back whatever thoughts she had about high-frequency hearing loss. My mother keeps a lot of her opinions inside, I think because she feels guilty about leaving me alone so much. Of course, she doesn't know about Evelyn; if anything, I'd like to be alone more often.

I picked up a mustard-colored T-shirt from a table display. It would have fit me perfectly if I were five foot ten and weighed eighty-five pounds.

"It's cute," my mother said uncertainly. She checked the price tag. "Forty dollars? For a T-shirt?" She checked my face. "You can have it if you love it."

Ah, the power of working-mother guilt.

I smirked. "It's fugly."

She relaxed. "It is, kind of."

I wandered farther back into the store and was looking at a cool but majorly overpriced sweatshirt when a familiar voice said, "Claire? Is that you?"

Of course Avon would be here. Avon was like a walking billboard for this place, the store's name plastered across her chest in a different color every day of the week.

It took me a second to recognize her. "What happened to your face?"

She touched her cheek—well, she touched the slab of makeup on her cheek, actually. "Me and Dayna got makeovers at Macy's? They were free, which was cool. Except then we had to buy makeup 'cause Dayna said they expect you to. My mom's gonna have a cow when she gets the credit-card bill, but—whatever."

Her eyes were lined in copper, and she was wearing too much blush. Her hair was blond (she'd discovered peroxide last year), long, and super-blow-dried straight. Still, she looked kind of good, I had to admit, if only because the chalky makeup covered her pimples. Her acne, which had blossomed in tandem with her breasts at the end of eighth grade, had gotten worse over the last year. Too bad her father wasn't a dermatologist.

My mother appeared at my side. "Avon? I didn't recognize you at first—you're getting so grown up!" My mother doesn't know that I hate Avon. Neither does Avon, because, to the best of her knowledge, there's no way I could know what she'd said about me back when we were supposed to be best friends.

"Are you here with your mom?" my mother asked.

"Nuh-uh," Avon said with a shudder that implied that only a loser would go to the mall with her mother. "I'm with Dayna? She's in me and Claire's grade? And she has an older sister who drives?"

"Oh, right. Dayna." My mother has no idea who Dayna is. I wish I could say the same. I could see her at the other end of the store checking out size 0 jeans, her long hair freshly bleached and blow-dried, her makeup a perfect match to Avon's. She pretended not to notice us, though I knew she and Avon would be doubled over with laughter as soon as my mother and I were out of sight.

"I don't like any of this stuff," I said, looking at my mother. "Let's go to Sears." Then I turned to Avon and made her hold my gaze. "I really like their boys' department." She looked frightened for an instant, as if she thought I could read her mind.

9

AVON'S AND MY FRIENDSHIP began with one birthday party and ended with another. The first was a joint celebration in our kindergarten classroom. My birthday fell on a Friday that year. My mother sent me to school with a cardboard box full of vanilla cupcakes. Avon appeared with her own box of cupcakes, also vanilla. We stared at the cupcakes and then at each other, amazed. We were turning six on the same day *and* we both liked vanilla? How could we help but be best friends?

The years that followed were a blur of play dates, sleepovers, and telephone conversations. I liked going to Avon's big house in the hills because her mother was always home and we could climb trees in the enormous backyard. Avon liked coming to my house because my mother was never home and the local woman who babysat let us eat junk food and watch TV.

I said we'd be college roommates someday. Avon said we would be each other's maids of honor. After that, we agreed, we'd buy houses next door to each other and have daughters the same age who would be best friends, just like us.

Things changed when we got to junior high school. Avon started going to the day spa for manicures and facials. (Sandyland doesn't have a movie theater, but it has a day spa. Life in a resort town can be weird.) I joined the junior-high swim team. Avon refused because she didn't want the chlorine to ruin her hair. She tried out for cheerleading but didn't make it. I said, "No big loss. Why would you want to be a cheerleader anyway?"

She said, "You just don't get it."

She was right. I didn't.

By eighth grade, Avon had begun hanging around with Ricki Chilter, another cheerleading reject, and Dayna Pynch, a squad alternate.

"You like them better than me," I joked one time. At least, I tried to sound like I was joking.

"Ricki and Dayna? Better than you?" She rolled her eyes. "You're just not around much anymore, you know. Swim team? All those practices and meets? Ring any bells?"

Looking back, Avon was already starting to get on my nerves, and she wore so many stinky floral products—perfumes and powders and hair sprays and deodorants—that I couldn't be in the same room with her without sneezing.

But still. She was my best friend. We were going to live next door to each other some day.

With Avon being born only two hours after me, it might seem inevitable that I'd switch into her body sooner or later. Her house in the hills was several miles away, though, so I figured I was safe.

But on the night of Dayna Pynch's slumber party (when Avon had told me she was going to her cousin's house in another town), she was right around the corner.

When we were little, Avon and I slept over at each other's house all the time, but once the switching began, I told her I'd started talking in my sleep and wouldn't want to keep her awake. I was so relieved when she accepted this lame excuse that it didn't occur to me to wonder why she didn't seem to mind.

The storm hit suddenly, violently, the rain pelting our roof. From the living room, my mother called to me to close the windows upstairs. I went from her bedroom to our shared bathroom to my room, pulling down the windows with shaking hands. I shut down my computer, much to Evelyn's dismay.

When all that was done, I sat on my bed and stared out the window. I hugged my knees to my chest as if I could hold my spirit inside. I trembled with fear of the unknown. Where would I end up tonight: in Kimmy's body? In Beanie's? I'd switched with each of them once at this point (not counting the time in science class). Well, okay, I hadn't really switched: I'd actually taken over their bodies and left them floating around in some unknown dimension while Evelyn, as me, raided the fridge.

Evelyn slipped over and sat down on the end of my bed. "Don't cry," she said. "I'm here."

I hadn't even known I was crying.

"You'll be back by morning," she said, her form becoming more distinct as the storm moved closer.

"Don't eat too much ice cream," I said, forcing a smile through my tears. "You gave me a stomachache last time."

She smiled back but didn't agree.

Then the lightning flashed and I woke up on the floor, sweating in a sleeping bag. I opened my eyes slowly. It was dark, but I could see two other forms on the floor.

"Hey, Avon, we thought you fell asleep."

Avon was here? I looked around, searching. Would she know me behind a stranger's eyes?

"Hey, Avon, you okay?" It was Ricki talking, I suddenly realized. Which meant that the other girl was . . . Dayna.

"What?" I said softly, testing my new vocal cords. "Yeah, I'm fine. I guess I just drifted off."

You know how it is when you hear your own voice on an answering machine or a video camera and it sounds nothing like you think it does? Well, that's how it felt hearing Avon's voice coming out of my mouth—her mouth. I recognized it, but it sounded different, lower or something.

"So, what were you going to say about Claire?" Dayna asked.

"Claire?" I said, my own name feeling odd on Avon's tongue.

"Did you see what she wore on the last day of school?" Ricki said.

"What she wears every day of school." Dayna snorted.

"Sweatpants," Ricki said. "My God."

Dayna laughed. "Avon said Claire buys all of her clothes at Sears—in the *boys'* department!"

Ricki gasped, her hand flying across her mouth.

"Didn't you say that, Avon?" said Dayna.

I stared at them.

"Avon?" Dayna said. Lightning flashed, reflecting against Dayna's braces. It looked like she had more braces than teeth.

Ricki and Dayna squealed at the lightning, then looked back at me—at Avon. I shrugged. "Sears has some cool clothes."

They paused, silent for a moment, then broke into a fit of giggles. "Avon, you are *so bad*," Ricki said. "You totally crack me up."

"I can't believe Claire doesn't know who her father is," Dayna said. I stared at her. Everyone knew who Dayna's father was. He was the McDonald's night manager who left his wife, Dayna's mother, for a twenty-year-old fry cook.

"Yeah, really," Ricki said. "And, like, how she stares at strange men to see if they look like her, like maybe they could be her father? It's totally creepy."

My breathing grew shallow. My palms were sweating. I had told Avon that I searched men's faces (in quick glances; I never stared) for clues: eyebrows shaped like mine or tiny clefts in their chins. I had told Avon and no one else.

"It's not as bad as her grandmother, though," Dayna said. "My mother said she went crazy and had to be put away. You think craziness could be catching? Like, genetically?"

I think I stopped breathing for a moment. I hadn't told anyone about my grandmother being sent to an insane asylum. Until that moment, I hadn't known myself. Was it even true, I wondered? Maybe Dayna was just saying that to be mean—well, meaner. But at some level, I knew that it must be true. First Avon's betrayal—now this. It was almost too much to process at once.

"What did you tell Claire about what we were doing tonight?" Dayna asked me. "Did she know about my birthday?" She turned to Ricki. "Claire kept asking Avon to hang out this weekend."

"Eew," Ricki said.

The lightning flashed again, and then the thunder came, a low rumble in the distance. The storm was moving away. "She told me she was going to her cousin's house," I said softly.

"What?" Ricki said, confused. "Claire was going to her cousin's? I didn't think she had any relatives."

"I mean, that's what I told her," I said. "I told Claire that I was going to my cousin's house." I swallowed hard, but the lump in my throat wouldn't go away. "I lied to Claire."

I tried to sleep, but Ricki and Dayna wouldn't stop talking—about who was too fat, too short, too loud, too shy. It was almost daybreak before their venom dried up. Finally, I closed my eyes and flew away from Avon's body—and from a friendship that, I knew now, had disappeared a long time ago.

10

It never gets normal, this business of leaving my body, but it has grown less terrifying, at least. We have developed a routine, Evelyn and I. She sits next to me in bed, her presence feeling like a cool draft. I close my eyes, take deep breaths, and wait for the inevitable.

After that awful switch with Avon, I asked Evelyn about the insane asylum. She stared at the wall for a long, silent time before admitting that it was true. "Though I wasn't crazy," she said. "Not for an instant."

"Was it really you in there?" I asked. "In . . . that place?" The mental hospital where Evelyn spent her last months was up in the hills, right at the edge of town. It has since been turned into condos.

She nodded sadly.

"Did they put you in there because of . . . the switching?" I asked, afraid to hear the answer.

"It was because I wasn't careful enough," she said. She wouldn't give any more details about the experience; she said it was too painful. And I didn't ask her about it either, because I was afraid of what I might learn.

Here's what Evelyn did tell me: As the years passed, she felt her spirit fading until she feared she would disappear altogether. It was getting harder and harder to see her daughter. It was like she saw everything through a thick ocean fog, the kind that creeps in during the middle of the night and refuses to burn off, even as the day grows long.

And then I was born. Evelyn doesn't know how it happened; she has no idea who my father is. My mother had never married, hadn't dated seriously in years. But then, so much had been lost in the fog.

Evelyn says my birth cleared the air for her, at least within the walls of our house. Outside, everything was still hazy.

"Switching is simply a fact of our lives, some genetic quirk," Evelyn has told me, time and time again. "It's what makes us different, like being left-handed or having red hair."

"I wish I could have red hair instead," I said one time.

"There's always Clairol," she replied.

The night after the mall trip, I spent the evening trying on my new clothes and deciding what to wear on the first day of school. I pictured Nate Jameson (I was good at that). Would he be more apt to notice me in my new jeans (which, okay, came from Sears, but from the juniors' department, at least) or in the cute skirt that I had found, miraculously, in Macy's?

56

Like it mattered. I could walk by Nate wearing nothing but a lacy black thong, and he'd still call me "dude."

I called Beanie to tell her about running into Avon at the mall. "She and Dayna got matching makeovers."

"There isn't enough makeup in the world . . . " Beanie said.

"I didn't even recognize her at first," I said. "She looked like a mime."

"If only she talked like one."

Beanie doesn't know how I found out what Avon said about me, of course; she just assumes I heard it secondhand. Beanie says Avon was always a nasty cow, and she always wondered why someone as nice as me would hang out with someone as transparently evil as Avon.

Beanie and I agreed to meet at the beach at ten o'clock the next morning to enjoy our last day of summer vacation. When I got off the phone, I looked back at the pile of clothes on my bed, with Fluffernutter sprawled on top. I buried my face in his stomach to hear him purr, then I shifted him off the clothes. No matter what outfit I chose, I'd be wearing white and orange fur on my first day of tenth grade. I finally settled on jeans and a top that looked like three shirts but was really just one.

That momentous decision out of the way, I crawled onto my bed and curled myself around Fluff. Just for a moment, I told myself. Right. I fell asleep on top of my covers, still wearing the new jeans and layered top.

When I woke up, I was all cramped and kind of cold. Fluffernutter had moved to the foot of my bed. I checked the clock: 4 A.M. My mother must have turned out my light, because it was dark. Evelyn wasn't in my room. I've told her it creeps me out when she watches me sleep. She was probably in the kitchen, messaging her MySpace friends. You'd expect death to be exhausting, but Evelyn never sleeps.

A full moon lit my room. I peeled off my clothes and shuffled across the new beige carpet. I couldn't see my pajamas in the darkness of the closet, so I groped inside for the light switch. I flipped the switch, and I saw a flash. Something stung my hand.

And then I was gone.

11

MY FIRST THOUGHT WASN'T, *Where am I?* or even, *Who am I?*, but rather, *Why?* Except for my very first switch, in science class, I'd only left my body during storms. But the night had been clear. And Mr. Pieteroski was nowhere to be seen.

I was *so* not in the mood for this right now.

I sat up in bed. It was a nice bed—big, comfortable. It had a shiny black headboard and a pouffy white comforter. Large square paintings hung on the walls. This did not look like a fifteen-year-old girl's room.

I examined my hands. The fingers were long and slender, the tips of the nails painted bright white. There was a name for this kind of manicure. Avon would know it.

I peeled the comforter away slowly. I was wearing an oversize, heather gray T-shirt. Under it, my legs flowed long and smooth and skinny. My toenails were bright pink.

The room was dark for such a bright night. I squinted, finally spotting a window. I slipped out of bed and crept over. The space between the window and the hillside was maybe two feet. No wonder it was so murky in there.

I listened carefully for sounds outside the room. When I didn't hear any, I turned on the light. There were no mirrors in the room, but I could see the paintings now. They were abstract, colorful. I didn't really like them, but I bet they cost a lot of money. The floors were some kind of pale wood, clean and gleaming. The walls were bright white.

This was the point at which I should have climbed back into the pouffy white bed, slipped back into sleep and into my own body. But it was kind of like when you wake up at night and you have to pee. You're torn: You want to go back to the comfort of sleep, but you're not sure if you can do it. Usually, it's best to just get that trip to the bathroom over with. It's like that when I switch. It's hard to fall back to sleep without knowing whose body I'm in. Once my curiosity is satisfied, it is much easier to conk out.

I was trying to decide whether to risk leaving the room to find a mirror when I noticed what must be a closet door. It was worth a try.

I opened it, not really expecting anything. When I saw the full-length mirror, I jumped and gasped.

It was her. Or, rather, I was her—the girl in the brown bikini, the girl Nate liked.

I touched the mirror with my slender fingers and gawked at the beautiful girl. She stared back. I cocked my head to one side. I smiled. I bent over until my thick blond hair almost touched the ground, and then I tossed the hair back over my head so it was even fuller and floatier than before.

"Darling," I said to the girl in the mirror. "You look fabulous."

I checked the digital clock on the nightstand. Only ten minutes had passed. Surely the girl wouldn't get up before, say, 5 A.M.? I certainly wouldn't. That gave me almost an hour to play.

I thought of Evelyn, back at my house. How much ice cream was she eating right now? Had she found the cookies that Mom hides in the cabinet over the refrigerator? It was bad enough that my mother worried about teenage pregnancies. Next she'd be lecturing me on eating disorders. Evelyn hadn't been in my room when I'd switched, but she couldn't have been far away. Surely she'd sensed something unusual and found her way to my room. Right?

The closet was stuffed with clothes. The girl had a little flippy miniskirt, royal blue with white pinstripes. I put it on with a tank top. It looked nothing like a school uniform. No school had ever been that cool. It felt like playing with a Barbie doll, only without the ratty hair and ruined knees. I wasn't just playing Barbie, though; I was *being* Barbie. Playing dress up had never been so much fun.

Next I tried on distressed jeans with a halter top, then supershort shorts with a little blouse that tied at the waist, then a billowy white sundress. I tried on the brown bikini—and then a blue one that, if possible, was even smaller.

There were flip-flops at the back of the closet, peachy pink with pink and orange flowers at the V. They were girly but funky—dainty but rubber. I loved them. I would never wear them

61

in my real life. They'd look ridiculous on me. But now . . . I slipped them on. The soles were thick and comfortable, and they made a satisfying slapping sound as I walked across the floor.

This was nothing like shopping with my mom.

While I played dress up, the numbers on the digital clock counted down the hour. At five o'clock, the sky outside was still black. Well, the thin space between the window and the hillside was dark, anyway. Surely another half hour wouldn't matter. Since I was the beautiful girl, I was probably in the Ice Cube House right now. *Just my luck,* I thought. *I finally switch into a house on the water, and I don't even get a room with a view.*

The novelty of the Barbie show wearing off, I tried to find something that looked bad. There was a pair of baggy pants that would have made my real body look stubby. They made the blond girl look urban and cool. I found some flat-front chinos buried in her pants drawer. *Aha!* I thought. *These will look boring!*

But they didn't. They were cut really low in the waist and flared out the tiniest bit at the ankle.

No matter what I did, I couldn't make the body look bad.

At five thirty, I packed it in. I slipped back into the enormous gray T-shirt and put the clothes back where I had found them. In her top drawer, amid belts, scarves, undies, and jewelry, I noticed a couple of greeting cards plus a bunch of business-size white envelopes, all addressed to "Larissa Hughes" in care of somebody named Krystal Calgrove. Krystal—and presumably, Larissa—lived about three hours away. I opened a red envelope. It was a birthday card dated March 10—surprise, surprise—and it said, "Happy fifteenth birthday to my girl. Love, Daddy."

There was a loose photograph in the drawer as well. It was of the girl—Larissa—in front of a giant redwood, leaning against a tall, pale man who looked kind of like her. He wore a baseball cap and a heather gray T-shirt, just like the one I was wearing now. Perhaps it was the same one. She wasn't dressed in any of her glamorous clothes. Instead, she wore faded jeans and sneakers. She was smiling.

Was her father here, I wondered? Probably not. From what I saw at the snack shack, she was a nanny. Too bad: I would have liked to meet him, to find out what it was like to have a father, if only for a few hours. But—whatever. He probably wouldn't have appreciated being woken up in the middle of the night, anyway.

I pulled at the gray T-shirt, which was easily the ugliest thing she owned. Then I smiled at the flawless face in the closet mirror before switching off the light and crawling back under the fluffy white comforter. I was on the verge of falling asleep when—

"I want juice!"

My eyes popped open. Standing at face level was one of the little blond boys I'd seen at the snack shack.

"What?" I said. My voice surprised me, even though I'd heard it before. It was nasal and high, not a beautiful-girl voice at all.

"I want juice!" He had sour morning breath. Who knew kids got such a thing?

"It's too early." I gasped. "Go back to sleep."

"If you don't get my juice, I'm going to scream!" His voice was getting higher, tighter.

I sat up and glared at him. "Listen, kid. I need my beauty sleep. You have no idea. Tell you what." I squinted at the clock. (*Don't panic*, I told myself. *There is still plenty of time*.) "Come back in half an hour—no, let's say an hour, just to be safe—and then I'll get up and get your juice and make you eggs or pancakes or whatever, but right now I'm going back to sleep." I turned away from him, curled up in a ball, and squeezed my eyes shut. (Sleep! I had to sleep!)

"AAAAAAAAAAHHHHHHH!"

I flipped back over. "Stop it!" I said. "You're going to wake everybody up!"

He tilted his pointy chin. "I told you I'd scream."

I narrowed my eyes. I've dealt with some brats before, but this kid was really starting to piss me off. "I'm not getting you any stinkin' juice."

"AAAAAAAAAHHHHHHH!" He closed his eyes and clenched his fists as he howled, then stopped for a moment to check my expression, which hadn't changed. He took a deep breath and pulled up his sharp little shoulders. "EEEEEEEEEEEE!"

"Are you going through all the vowels?" I asked when he quieted down. "The next one is *I*, in case you're wondering."

He looked at me, bewildered. "Where is my mommy?"

"I don't know. Sleeping?" I, too, was surprised that his mother hadn't come running to see what was wrong.

"MOMMMMEEEEEEEE!"

I was all set to remind him that we were done with the *E*s and it was time to move on to the *I*s when I noticed that his tears were real. "Don't cry," I said.

"I want Mommeeeeeee!"

I moaned. "Okay. You win. If I get you juice, will you stop crying?" He nodded, too distraught to speak.

"And will you go back to bed after that?"

He nodded again.

And I was stupid enough to believe him.

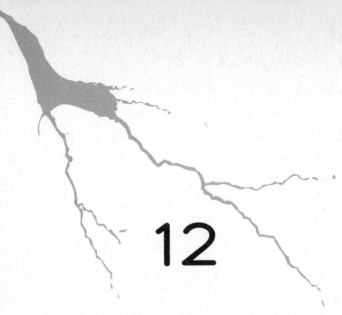

12

Juice Boy was Cameron. He was five. I found that out by doing a little investigative work as he finished his second glass of juice.

"How old are you again?"

"You know how old I am," he whined. Cameron's voice was like a siren.

"I forgot."

He scowled. "If you forgot, you're stupid."

"Oh, now I remember. You're four."

"I'm not four! Prescott is four! I'm five, and I hate you!" He jumped out of his chair and clenched his little hands into fists. His face grew red. "Mommmeeeeee! Larissa is being mean!"

This had to be the cruddiest babysitting job in Sandyland, if not in all of North America.

At least serving as Cameron's juice waitress meant I got to see more of the Ice Cube House. There were three floors in the big concrete box. Larissa and the boys slept on the bottom level, which backed up to the hillside on one end and led out to the lawn on the other. There appeared to be a third bedroom down there as well, but the door was closed. The downstairs was dark because the upstairs deck hung over the sliding glass door. The main floor, which had stairs going up to another level, was one big kitchen-and-living-room combo. The walls and furniture were bright white, the counters and table were stainless steel, and the floor was the same fugly gray concrete as the outside of the house. It made Beanie's sterile house look cozy in comparison. It would have been a horrible room if not for the view. The far wall was all glass, opening onto the huge deck, with sky and sea providing a spectacular and ever-changing backdrop.

Six o'clock came, then six thirty. The ocean outside changed from black to silver. The inky sky turned a powdery blue. I tried to go back to bed. Cameron turned on his siren whine. Still no Mommy.

At 6:45, Prescott came stomping into the living room. He was shorter than Cameron, more solid, and meaner looking. If Cameron was Juice Boy, then Prescott was Chocolate Milk Boy. But he didn't tell me that. He just asked for (demanded) milk. Presumably the chocolate part was understood—which was why he was perfectly justified in throwing the white milk that I handed him across the room and screaming, "You're stupid! I hate you!"

It's always nice when two brothers can agree on something.

Maybe I could nap later, I thought, on my hands and knees on the cold concrete floor, cleaning up the milk with a wad of paper towels. And maybe Evelyn could nap later too. Surely Evelyn

67

would cover for me. Surely—*surely*—she had gotten into my body in time.

At seven, a short, stout woman in a maid's uniform came clomping up the stairs.

"Morning, Consuela!" Cameron squealed, all sweetness and sunshine.

"How are my angels? My angels happy today, huh?"

The boys ran to her and wrapped their arms around her thick waist. "I want waffles!" Prescott snapped. "Larissa won't make them!" Prescott had never asked me to make waffles. Prescott had said he wasn't hungry yet.

"Larissa, she don't know how to cook," Consuela said, stroking Prescott's golden hair. "Larissa, she too busy looking in the mirror."

My jaw dropped. I was all set to defend myself—or, even better—to whip up the best waffles these demon children had ever tasted—when I remembered that I was not Claire, I was Larissa. And maybe Larissa deserved Consuela's contempt.

Fifteen minutes later, when Consuela put a platter of waffles on the table, I pulled out a chair to sit, and I noticed that there were only two places set. (Even the plates were white and square and ugly.) I walked over to the counter as quietly as I could, wondering where the rest of the square plates were kept. I hadn't looked for anything beyond the boys' plastic cups.

"What you want?" Consuela asked sharply.

"Just a plate. I can get it myself." I checked her eyes, hoping they'd flit to the appropriate cabinet.

"What you gonna do with a plate?" she asked.

68

I thought, *Break it in half and use it to slit my wrists.* "Um, I was hoping I could, well—I'm hungry."

She blinked in astonishment. "You going to eat breakfast?"

"If it's okay."

She snorted. "Sure, it's okay. I just never seen you eat breakfast before."

Consuela's waffles weren't as good as the ones I make (I use mashed bananas), but I put away four. Switching bodies works up an appetite.

At eight o'clock, Cameron and Prescott's mother finally came down the steps from the upper level. She was shorter than Larissa but almost as skinny, her hair six shades of blond. She wore black yoga pants over a sky blue leotard.

"Mommeeeee!" Cameron shrieked, running across the floor. Prescott glanced up and then went back to jabbing his place mat with a fork.

"Hello, my darling," the mother said, bending over and opening her arms to Cameron. "Watch Mommy's makeup."

She began to straighten, but Cameron's arms remained locked around her neck. "Okay, darling, let Mommy stand up. Herbal tea, please, Consuela?" She took hold of Cameron's hand and pried it away from her neck. "Good morning, Larissa," she said.

"Good morning." I smiled carefully. Mommy's face looked sallow under her makeup, as if she hadn't slept well. I wondered what Mommy's real name was and what I was supposed to call her.

She settled into the chair next to mine and sighed. "What a night. That bed is so uncomfortable. I'm about ready to complain to the rental company."

Ah—so they were just renting the Ice Cube House.

"Maybe Cameron's bed is uncomfortable too," I said. "He got up kind of early."

"Oh, Cameron." She rolled her eyes. "He has yet to master sleeping through the night." At that, Cameron came over and tried to climb into her lap. "Not now, my lovey," she said, batting away Cameron's scrawny limbs. "Mommy's about to have her tea and she wouldn't want to spill on you. Consuela? How's that tea coming along?"

"Almost ready, Missus Sealy."

Mrs. Sealy turned to Prescott. "How's my little Presie this morning?" she asked in a baby voice.

"I want to go to the beach," he growled, without looking up from his mutilated place mat.

"Of course you can go to the beach, Peanut," she cooed. "Larissa will take you after breakfast."

"I want to go swimming," he said, still stabbing.

"Daddy will take you in the ocean when he comes this weekend."

"I want to go swimming *now*."

Mrs. Sealy sighed—actually, it sounded more like a moan— and closed her eyes for a moment. When she opened them, she said, "You know Larissa can't take you into the ocean, Presie."

"But, *why?*"

"We've been through this before." She smiled at me gently.

"Larissa can't take you into the ocean because Larissa can't swim."

Mrs. Sealy left soon after that, carrying her herbal tea in an enormous travel cup. "I finally tracked down a yoga studio, thank God," she told me. "I've been feeling so off balance, so uncentered lately, probably just not taking good enough care of myself." She put a twenty-dollar bill on the stainless steel countertop. "This should cover lunch for you and the boys in case I don't make it back in time. And don't forget their sunscreen—at least fifteen minutes before they go outside."

She kissed the boys good-bye, grabbed her keys, and called out, "See you in a bit!"

Cameron sprinted after her. I practically had to hold him down to keep him from getting run over by her silver luxury SUV. He had tears in his eyes.

"Don't worry," I said. "Mommy will come home soon."

He blinked at me, as if he'd forgotten for a moment that I existed. "I hate you!" he said.

"How can you hate me? You hardly even know me." I was fishing.

He stared down the road until the SUV disappeared, and then he turned to me with a scowl. "I've known you for, like, a hundred years. I've known you since before I was born."

"That's not possible." Like I was one to talk about possible.

"My mom and your mom are friends! So it is too possible!" And then he started to cry. Again.

But for now, Cameron was the least of my problems. I knew

where Larissa's body was, but what about my own? I had to go see Evelyn—or, more precisely, to see myself. I kept trying to convince myself that she'd made it up to my room in time, but I wasn't so sure—though I couldn't imagine that Larissa would have much use for my body anyway.

I settled the boys in front of a DVD and asked Consuela to keep an eye on them while I went out for a short while.

"Why? You got a date?" she asked.

I rolled my eyes. "Yeah, that's it. I got a smokin' hot date."

In the bedroom, I pulled out a pair of sneakers (plaid, Converse, super cute). I'd thrown on a pair of gym shorts when Cameron first got me up, so there was no real reason I couldn't go out "as is," in the baggy gray T-shirt. But why leave the house looking merely pretty when I could be spectacular?

It took me only a moment to choose between a black halter top and a little orange blouse that tied at the waist. I went with the blouse. It looked just right with Larissa's faded denim miniskirt.

I didn't bother with makeup or earrings. That would have been overkill.

I knew I was in trouble the minute I stepped into my yard. Evelyn—or a vague outline of Evelyn—was sitting on the front porch steps, smoking her cigarette.

"Oh, no!" I gasped.

Evelyn looked at me blankly for a minute and then smiled when she realized who I was. "Don't start with me," she said, flicking an imaginary ash onto the grass. "Smoking is one of the few pleasures I have left."

"Not that," I said. "You. Here. Sitting on the steps. If you're here, who's . . . ?" I looked up at my bedroom window.

"I think her name is Larissa." She looked me up and down. "I wondered what she looked like. Pretty. No wonder she's so helpless. What happened?"

"I don't know. One moment I was in my closet, flipping the light switch, and the next thing you know, I'm in this monster house on the beach. It doesn't make sense. I remember seeing the moon outside my window, and the room had that nasty new-carpet smell, and— That's it!" I snapped my fingers.

"What?"

"It was the switch! The switch made me switch!"

"You lost me."

"You know that new carpet Mom is so jazzed about? I shuffled across it in bare feet and then hit the light. Must have generated some static electricity."

"That's what your mother gets for buying a polyester carpet." Evelyn sighed. "If only I had lived. I would have taught her to appreciate quality. But I still don't get it. Didn't you go to sleep last night?"

I shook my head. "I tried to, but this little kid woke me up." She didn't need to know about my mini fashion show. Suddenly I pictured Larissa, poking through my closet. And then I imagined my mother coming home at the end of the day. "This is a disaster!"

"Now, now. Don't overreact." Evelyn gave me a limp-wristed, no-big-deal wave. "You'll be fine once you go to sleep. For now, I've got everything under control. Larissa thinks she's having a dream. A really long, strange dream. She's just lying around, whimpering and asking if she's going to wake up soon."

"But what is she doing in my body? Why didn't you get there first?"

"You didn't exactly give me a warning. I was downstairs. And even though that was a lot closer to you than Princess Pathetic, her electrical pull was stronger than mine because she is—you know. Alive." She rolled her eyes.

"But didn't you sense something? Some sudden change in electrical forces? You must have had a few seconds, at least. Why didn't you rush upstairs?"

Evelyn leveled her gray gaze at me. "I was Instant Messaging Roger, and we were having a moment."

"Who's Roger?"

"He's a gentleman friend. An American living in Denmark. Very lonely. Very nice. I couldn't just abandon him in mid-sentence."

"So that's what you've been doing hour after hour on the Internet? Hooking up with some poor guy who thinks you're alive?"

"I'm entitled to a little happiness," Evelyn said, tugging on her long braid.

"But you were supposed to protect me!"

She pulled herself up straight. "Not everything is about you, Claire."

"Aargh!" I buried my face—Larissa's face—in my hands. In Larissa's hands. "Okay. Here's what we're going to do. Wait a few hours and then give her some Benadryl. Let's say three o'clock?"

74

"Why Benadryl?"

"It always knocks me out. Since she's in my body, it should knock her out too. I'll go back and take the boys to the beach, really wear them out so we can all take naps. I should be back in my body by dinner, and Larissa can wake up from her dream."

"One itty-bitty problem," Evelyn said.

"What?"

"I don't have a body."

"Your point being?"

"I can't exactly get past the childproof cap on the Benadryl bottle. Or any cap, for that matter."

"Ugh." I wrinkled Larissa's pert nose. "I'll take care of it."

The Benadryl bottle was on the bottom shelf of the medicine cabinet, between a tube of extra-strength Clearasil and some ear drops. I shook a couple of pink tablets onto my palm, and then I added a couple more. Evelyn appeared behind me.

"Just tell her to come get these." I put the tablets on the counter next to the sink, along with a glass of water. "Tell her they're diet pills."

"What if she won't take them?"

"She'll gobble them up. Believe me."

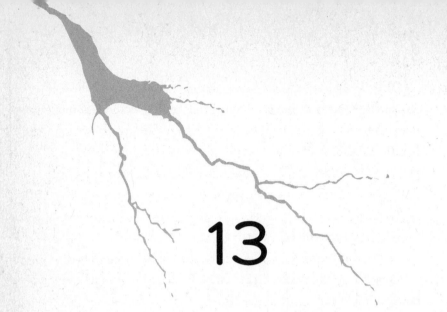

13

THERE WAS NO MISTAKING A BEACH OUTING with Cameron and Prescott for a dream—a nightmare, maybe. First came the bathing-suit battle. Cameron wanted to wear his shark bathing suit. But the real Larissa hadn't hung his shark bathing suit up properly the day before, and it smelled. I suggested he wear the orange trunks instead.

"I want to wear my shark suit!"

Fine. So he smelled.

Next came Prescott, who didn't want to wear a bathing suit at all because it was much more fun to run around buck naked, penis in hand, yelling, "I got a pee-pee! I got a pee-pee!" As it turned out, Prescott was not telling us that he *had* a pee-pee. He was telling us that he had to *go* pee-pee. Funny, the difference a couple of words can make. Ha, ha. Hilarious.

Once I got that mess cleaned up (I'll spare you the details), I sent the boys off to bug Consuela while I put on my bathing suit.

Okay. I admit it. I took a little longer getting dressed than was absolutely necessary. Brown bikini or blue? The brown covered more, believe it or not, but I'd already seen it on Larissa—the old Larissa, that is. I wanted something new, something *mine*. So I put on the blue. But then I worried that it showed too much of, well, pretty much everything. So I tried on the brown suit— which brought up the old Larissa/new Larissa issues. So I went back to the blue suit (along with a delicate silver anklet), but I covered up with the oversized gray T-shirt Larissa wore to bed.

Cameron and Prescott were in the kitchen sucking on juice boxes when I finally appeared. Consuela was nowhere to be seen.

"Okay, your sunscreen," I said. "Where is it?"

"We got it already," Cameron said. "Consuela did it."

That was one less thing to worry about, at least.

We spread our towels on the sand in front of the rock wall, right below the house. I sat down, took off the big gray T-shirt, and spread suntan lotion over my endless legs, scrawny arms, and unbelievably flat tummy. There was a lot of surface to cover: The blue bikini was teeny. Once I convinced the boys to stop climbing on the rocks (I told them it was illegal and they might get thrown in jail), they started running to the edge of the surf and then back—to the edge and back again. If they kept this up for a couple more hours, I'd have it made.

But the water splashed Cameron in the face and he started to wail. "My face is wet!" Of course, in Cameron-speak, "wet" went on for minutes: "WEH-uh-EH-uh-EH-uh-ET!" The kid should've had a flashing red light on his head.

"We're at the beach," I said. "Water happens."

He finally settled down enough to dig in the sand. He'd filled half a bucket—not a terribly big bucket, even—when he got a grain of sand in his eye. "My eye!" He wailed, clawing his face with his (sandy) hands and making it worse. "My eye-aye-aye-aye-aye!"

This was right about the time that Prescott discovered the joy of seagulls, or rather, the joy of throwing rocks at seagulls.

So I said, "Keep crying, Cameron. That's good—your tears will wash the sand out. STOP IT, PRESCOTT! No, Cameron, I can't call your mommy, she's at yoga—PRESCOTT, LEAVE THE SEAGULLS ALONE! Cameron! Mommy will be back soon and then—PRESCOTT! NO!"

Prescott didn't manage to hit a seagull. He did, however, graze the shoulder of a big, scary tattooed guy jogging down the beach.

"Ow!" the guy said, grabbing his shoulder.

I jumped up and ran over to the jogger, fully prepared to be chewed out. "I'm so sorry!" I said. "I wouldn't have let him throw rocks, but his brother got sand in his eye and—"

I stopped talking because the man was looking at me in the strangest way, his eyes all buggy. There was blood dripping down his tattooed shoulder, the red blurring the lines of his blue tattoo, and then all of a sudden he was . . . smiling? How could that be?

"Are you okay?" I asked, thinking: *Are you crazy?*

"I'm great," he said, still smiling, still bleeding, still . . . leering.

"Oh. Good."

I nodded at his shoulder. "You should probably wash that off." My skinny arms crossed in front of my concave belly, but the bikini didn't allow for much modesty. I wished I had left the gray shirt on.

"Maybe you can wash it off for me," he said, moving a little closer.

I stepped back, right onto a shell. "Ouch!" I stumbled and looked at him with what was surely fear.

He held up his hands in a peace gesture. One of his hands, the one that had been holding his shoulder, was smeared with blood. "Hey," he said. "Just kidding."

I didn't respond.

He'd stopped smiling. He shook his head, irritated now, and grimaced, finally, at his shoulder. He swore under his breath. Then he gave me one last long look and walked away.

My legs shaking, I settled back on the towel next to Cameron, who was still sniffling, though not crying as much as before.

"I'm hungry," Prescott announced.

I looked at the back of the bloody tattooed man. He'd started jogging again and was getting farther away by the second.

"Five minutes," I said, pulling the gray T-shirt over my head.

"I'm hungry!" Prescott's angry growl was almost as bad as Cameron's fire-siren whine.

I glared at Prescott. He glared back. I looked away first. "Five minutes," I muttered. I saw something out of the corner of my eye and turned. It was Cameron, scaling the boulders, working his way up to the "Keep Off Rocks" sign.

"Cameron!" I yelled.

He climbed higher. Prescott scurried over to join him.

"No!"

Prescott turned around, one hand still on a boulder.

"Five minutes are up," I said, although of course they weren't. "Let's have lunch."

By the time we reached the snack shack, I was so hot from the walk that beads of sweat slithered down my back. My face felt like it was glowing. The ocean shone blue and inviting. I'd have given anything to jump in, but since Larissa had never learned to swim, I was stuck on the hot sand.

Ryan smiled when I approached the counter. "You're back," he said.

I narrowed my eyes and kept my mouth turned down. "We'll have two hot dogs with lemonade."

"I want a milk shake!" Cameron squealed.

I swung my head around. "Yeah? Well, I want a week in Maui. *Alone.*" I turned back to Ryan, pleased and surprised that I'd shut Cameron up for once.

Ryan leaned on the counter and gazed at me. He had one of those peach-fuzz mustaches, and it was studded with perspiration. "And what can I get for you?"

I crossed my arms around my waist. My ribs poked through the T-shirt. "I'll have a double cheeseburger. With everything."

"Okay." He wrote it down.

I glanced down at my legs: skinny, skinny, skinny. "And an order of onion rings. Large."

"Okay."

"And to drink, let's see." Another bead of sweat slithered down my back. "A milk shake. Chocolate. Jumbo."

"Wow," he said. "I like a girl with an appetite."

80

I ground my teeth together. "Well, you're out of luck, because I like a guy with a personality."

He looked so hurt that I actually felt bad for about one one-thousandth of a second. He told me how much money I owed, and I gave him Mrs. Sealy's twenty-dollar bill.

"I'm actually pretty nice when you get to know me," he said, handing over my change. Did this guy ever give up?

"That'll never happen," I said.

We ate at the picnic table. Larissa's deprived little stomach started to hurt after half a burger, but I soldiered on, mostly for Ryan's benefit. At one point, I felt grease spill down my chin and I left it there on purpose. I was on a mission to make Larissa look gross.

I had to stop after a couple of onion rings and a few sips of the shake: I was in serious pain by then, and I didn't want to risk vomiting, no matter whose body I was in (even though it would have accomplished the grossness mission). The boys asked for some of my shake. I lied and said I finished it all. Something— either the heat or my beauty or the kids—was making me mean. What shocked me was that I was getting away with it.

For the first time ever, Nate saw me before I saw him. Okay, that's not strictly true. Nate saw Larissa before I saw him. I heard someone pop out of the surf as Prescott, Cameron, and I began our long walk back to the Ice Cube House and turned to see Nate looking away from me, pretending like he hadn't seen me at all. He wiped the water out of his eyes. His blond curls, dripping with ocean water, framed his tanned face.

Before I could do or say anything, Cameron had run over to him.

"Are you a lifeguard?" Cameron asked him—though it took me a moment to realize who was talking. I'd never heard Cameron speak without whining before.

"Not yet," he said. "This summer I worked at a camp, teaching kids to be better ocean swimmers. But next summer, I'll be sitting right up there." He pointed to a lifeguard tower. I thought, *Good. Now I know where to spread my towel.*

"Hi." I smiled. Nate always made me smile. "We met yesterday. Well, we didn't really meet, but I saw you. At the snack shack."

His face, speckled with ocean drops, flushed pink.

"You were with those two girls," I added.

"What girls?"

"I'm Larissa," I said, because I didn't know what else to say.

"Nate," he added, finally cracking a smile.

"So you're not a lifeguard," Cameron said.

"Do you little guys like the ocean?" Nate asked, squatting down to Cameron's level.

"We're not allowed in the water because Larissa can't swim," Prescott volunteered.

Nate blinked up at me in surprise.

"Of course I can swim," I said, wondering if that were true. "Just not very well. Not good enough to go into the ocean." Beyond the wave break, the yellow swim float bobbed gently. It was covered with people. If it weren't for this body-switching nonsense, I'd be out at that float in fifteen strokes. Of course, if it weren't for the body switching, Nate wouldn't be talking to me.

Nate straightened. "I could teach you." He snuck a peek at my face and then, embarrassed, looked at the ground.

"I'd like that," I said. "The thing is, I'm leaving soon." I swallowed hard, the pain in the pit of my stomach suddenly unrelated to my cheeseburger.

He wasn't giving up. "How about a lesson now, then? I mean, if you want."

I stared at him for a moment. Then I checked the boys, who were watching Nate with wide eyes.

A wave slid up the beach and splashed my ankles. It felt so good. "I'm supposed to be babysitting," I mumbled.

Nate squatted back down to the boys' level. "How about if I give Larissa a quick lesson, and you guys watch us? Then, afterward, I'll give you each a ride on a boogie board."

Cameron and Prescott nodded in unison, silent for once.

"The lifeguard's a friend of mine," Nate told me. "They can sit right in front of his chair."

I felt both embarrassed and excited to take off the gray T-shirt. Nate did his best not to stare, but I caught him looking me up and down, almost as if he couldn't control his eyeballs. Mostly, he tried hard to look in my eyes, even though they were Larissa's least impressive feature.

Pretending I couldn't swim wasn't as hard as I thought it would be. My thoughts went something like this:

Nate is so hot. Oh, my God—a wave! Will the bikini stay on? Yikes! Grab the top! No, the bottom! That was close. . . . Cute. He is so cute. And nice. He's got that one dimple, just on his left cheek, and—oh, my God! Another wave! Hold the suit!

We stayed near the spot where the waves were breaking, about waist deep. The surf was unusually calm, even by Sandyland's standards. He taught me to dive under a breaking wave, to float on my stomach, to paddle with my head up. When a rogue wave knocked me over, he held my arms gently and said, "Are you okay?"

I nodded, coughing a bit, and drawing out the moment more than was strictly necessary. The weird thing was, the wave really did knock me over; I wasn't faking it. Scrawny arms and tooth-pick legs may look nice, but there was no denying it: Larissa was a ninety-pound weakling.

I would have stayed in the water longer, but Nate noticed me shivering and said I should warm up. Strike two for Larissa's beautiful body: It lacked insulation. My teeth chattered uncontrollably.

"You have an amazing feel for the water," Nate told me. "It's hard to believe you've never been in the ocean before."

As I settled on the sand, I saw Beanie sitting nearby, frowning at her watch. It was all I could do not to call out to her, to run over and say, "You're never going to believe this, but . . ."

Beanie was alone. Of course she was: She and I had agreed to meet there at ten o'clock, and it was almost noon. I'd have to think of some excuse before I saw her at school tomorrow, as much as I hated to lie.

As she hugged her knees to her chest, Beanie caught me staring at her. I smiled. She glared and looked away. A few towels away, a group of guys—men, really, probably out of high school—gawked at me. I spun back to face the water and sat down. I hugged my knees to my chest, just as Beanie had done, and watched Nate and the boys.

He was at the water's edge, giving them a lecture on water safety. "Until you're older and a really strong swimmer, you should never go into the water without an adult. And no one should ever go into the ocean without someone else around, even if they're the best swimmer in the world." He warned them of the dangers of getting too far out, of getting too tired, of getting too cold.

"But you can swim alone," Cameron said. "You're almost a lifeguard."

"Sure, I can swim alone," Nate said. "But I'd never swim without someone on the beach. I could get hurt and need help getting back to shore. Or I could get caught in a riptide."

"What's a riptide?" Prescott asked.

"A riptide is this really strong current that pulls you out to sea. You can't see it. And you can't fight it. All you can do is let it take you out, then swim far down the shore until you can get back to the beach. But you don't need to worry about that right now. Right now we need to get you some life jackets."

"I'm not wearing a stupid life jacket!" Prescott snapped, his true nature finally showing through.

"Okay." Nate shrugged. "Then you're not going in the water."

Prescott scrunched his face and bit his lip. Then he looked down at the sand and dug a little hole with his toe. "I guess I'll wear a life jacket," he mumbled.

Nate borrowed a couple of tiny life jackets from the lifeguard. Then he took the boys into the water, one at a time, well ahead of the wave break, and pulled them on the boogie board.

"Ouch," Cameron said when Nate put a hand on his shoulder.

"Sorry, little guy. Did I grab you too hard?" He peered at Cameron's shoulder. "Uh-oh—looks like you're getting a sunburn."

Prescott sat on the sand next to me, awaiting his turn. His formerly white arms glowed pink. So did his legs. And his face.

"Prescott? You did say that Consuela put sunscreen on you, right?"

"I forget," he said, without looking at me.

Cameron forgot too.

"You wouldn't say that Consuela put lotion on you if she hadn't, would you?" I asked stupidly as he took the spot next to me on the sand.

"I want another boogie-board ride," he whined. "I wanna go back in the water."

"Look at me, Cameron," I said, placing a hand on his arm.

"Ouch!"

When Prescott got out of the water, Nate asked me if I wanted to try the boogie board. My chest actually ached, I wanted to do it so badly. But it was getting late, and I couldn't risk missing my nap. Besides, I had to get the boys out of the sun—and fast.

"This has been really fun." I stood up and brushed sand off of my long, long legs.

"It really has." He smiled shyly. "Can I see you again? Maybe to swim, or—whatever."

I swallowed hard. "I'd like that. Really. The thing is, I won't be here much longer. Tomorrow I'll be gone."

He nodded and fiddled with the string on his swim trunks. "I don't know if you can get out tonight, but a bunch of my friends and me, we like to come down to the beach after sunset. Have a bonfire, hang out, that sort of thing. So, if you're not doing anything . . ."

I blinked at him. A bonfire? With lots of kids? And no one had ever invited me? Remembering who I was—or who I was supposed to be—I shook my head. "I don't think I can make it. But thanks. For everything."

He nodded sadly. "Maybe next summer."

"You never know," I said. Because, really, I never did.

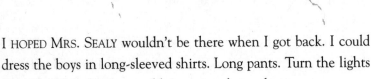

14

I HOPED MRS. SEALY wouldn't be there when I got back. I could dress the boys in long-sleeved shirts. Long pants. Turn the lights down low. Maybe she wouldn't notice the sunburns.

Or maybe she would.

"Oh, my God!" She gasped. "What happened?"

"A day at the beach," I said lamely.

"You were supposed to put sunblock on! Fifteen minutes before they went outside! I told you!"

Cameron began to cry. "Mommy, it hurts! My skin hurts!" He stumbled across the room, his arms outstretched.

Faker, I thought. He didn't complain once on the walk home.

"Oh, my little Cammie!" Mrs. Sealy cooed. "You poor little sweetheart." He was all set to throw himself into her arms when she said, "No, no, darling! You're covered in sand. You'll get Mommy dirty."

Cameron stopped in his tracks and looked down, his tears falling on the ground.

"The boys told me that Consuela put sunscreen on them," I said evenly.

"And did you check with Consuela?"

"No."

"Well, then."

It was silent for a moment save for Cameron's sniffling. According to the nickel-plated clock on the wall, it was a quarter of three, which meant I had a date with unconsciousness in fifteen minutes. I felt kind of bad for the real Larissa, having to deal with this mess when she woke up.

"I need to shower," I announced.

"The boys need baths," Mrs. Sealy said.

I looked at them. They were seriously red. Prescott was sitting on the ground, zoning out. He looked like he might fall asleep right there. I turned to their mother and held her gaze. "They certainly do," I said.

Back in my room, I didn't bother showering. There wasn't time. I took one last look in the mirror. I wasn't as pink as the boys (I'd used sunscreen on myself, at least), but Larissa's face glowed in a way that made it even more beautiful than before. Her masses of blond hair were wild and tangled. I smiled at my reflection. I'd never be so beautiful again.

There wasn't time to change out of the little blue bikini or the soggy oversized T-shirt. I lay down on top of the bed. Too bad I didn't have a view. It would have been nice to spend my last moments there gazing at the ocean.

"Good night, Larissa," I whispered. "And good-bye."

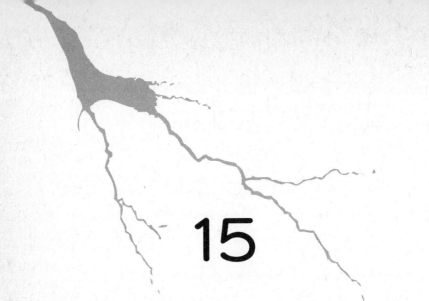

15

I THINK I WAS DREAMING—it was a nice dream, something about Nate—when I heard the knocking. There were three knocks: *tap-tap-tap*. Then four, louder this time: *tap-TAP, tap-TAP*.

I buried my face in the overfilled pillow and breathed in the scent of laundry detergent. If it was my mother at the door, she'd peek in on me, and then she'd tiptoe away and let me rest.

The knocking came harder this time: *BAM! BAM! BAM!*

There was a smell mixed with the laundry detergent. Bleach. My sheets at home were colored. Bleach would ruin them.

Finally, she gave up on knocking and opened the door. I sat up and stared at her, hoping for one brief, futile moment that it was my mother, home from work.

It wasn't my mother. My mother had no idea where I was.

Maybe I was never really asleep at all.

"Larissa," Mrs. Sealy said. She cleared her throat.

I looked down at my legs: long. Checked my fingers: manicured. Fingered my hair: blond.

It was true: I was still Larissa.

"Yes, Mrs. Sealy," I said.

She let out a sigh and walked across the room, a big glass of white wine in her hand. It was twenty minutes past three.

She stood next to my bed and pointed to the spot next to me. "You mind?" I shook my head. She sat on the bed, sighed again, and took a long drink of her wine.

"I always wanted a daughter," she announced. She smiled. At least, her mouth smiled. The top half of her face didn't move at all.

"Oh," I said, thinking, *And your point is?*

"Consuela is bathing the boys," she said. She paused, like I was supposed to respond to that. When I didn't, she said, "Consuela told me you went out this morning."

I was trying to come up with a good excuse when it struck me how Larissa would respond to that question: I shrugged.

"Your mother called," she said, and for a brief moment I thought she meant my real mother. "About a half an hour, forty-five minutes ago. You just missed her."

She wasn't talking about my real mother, of course. The caller was Larissa's mother, a complete stranger. Not knowing what to say, I shrugged again.

"The cruise ship was about to leave Mykonos," she continued. "So she won't have cell-phone service again for three days."

Now I was confused. I mean, even more confused. "Why did she—I mean, my mother—wait to call me until she was about to leave?"

She ignored the question. "Were you with your father this morning?"

My father? Wasn't he with my mother? I mean, Larissa's mother?

I shook my head. "No."

"Your mother was wondering. He's been so difficult about the whole custody thing. But your mother's got you for the whole summer. That's what the court decided, and he knows it. He'll see you in October."

My eyes shot to the drawer where I had found the photo of Larissa and her father.

Mrs. Sealy took another drink of her wine. The glass was huge. "You know, Larissa, you need to grow up a little, stop thinking about yourself all the time. Your mother has made so many sacrifices, and you just keep acting out." She looked at the ceiling. "Though your father didn't help, that's for sure. The way he's always spoiled you, let you do whatever you wanted. It's time for you to take some responsibility for your actions. Time to give your poor mother a break."

I was about to ask what kind of a break Larissa's mother needed beyond a cruise in the Greek Isles when I noticed the digital clock on top of the nightstand. If I didn't fall asleep soon, I'd be stuck in Larissa's body until morning.

"You're right," I said. "I'm wrong. Not for seeing my father, because I didn't, but for everything. I'm sorry. I think I just need some sleep."

"Maybe later." She stood up and smoothed out her slacks. "Right now I'm going out, so I'll need you to keep an eye on the boys." Her eyes flicked over me; I was still in the little bathing suit. "Perhaps you can take a quick shower and get dressed first."

"You're going out?" I gasped. "But you just got home!"

"I got home over an hour ago," she said evenly. "You weren't here."

Because you made me take your kids to the beach, I thought, but I kept my mouth shut.

I had ten minutes to shower and change into shorts and a T-shirt—uninspired but there was no time to spare. Then I was back on duty. The boys refused to take naps. That shouldn't have surprised me, but it did, somehow. Finally, I settled them on the white couch with sippy cups and blankets and turned on the Disney Channel. I slipped back to my room and dove onto the bed. I shut my eyes and lay there for maybe five minutes before Cameron came to tell me he had spilled milk on the couch (which he pronounced "cow-ouch").

"But it was a no-spill cup!"

He wrinkled his nose and swallowed a sob. "I took the top off."

"No big deal. Milk's white, the couch is white," I said, forgetting for a moment that the boys drank only chocolate milk.

Once I'd blotted the spilled milk, flipped over the couch cushion and fought with Cameron over whether or not he could have another chocolate milk (he won), I headed back to my room.

Consuela was pulling the sheets off of my bed.

I yelped. She gave me a dirty look and then went back to yanking off the sheets.

"I was going to take a nap," I explained.

"This late?" she said. It was 5:20. Time was running out. My

93

mother left work at six o'clock. I had to get to sleep—and get back into my own body— and I had to do it soon.

"Where are the extra sheets?" I asked. "I'll make up the bed."

"No extras," she said.

"None?"

"Is a rental."

She dumped the sheets in a laundry basket and hauled it into the hall. I smoothed the comforter back on top of the bed. I was about to lie down when Consuela reappeared with the vacuum cleaner and a mean smirk. She turned on the vacuum. It was a nice machine, a lot quieter than the one we have at home (I've been stuck with vacuum duty since I was ten). Still, it was clear: I would not be napping.

"I need to go out," I announced.

She narrowed her eyes. "You got a date?" I glared at her. You'd think she'd get some new material.

I put a hand on my abdomen and winced. "Cramps. I need to go to the drugstore. The boys are just watching TV."

She shrugged. "Mrs. Sealy, she don't like you leaving."

"I won't be gone long."

Evelyn was pacing in front of my house. "Where have you been?"

"I couldn't sleep. I tried, but they wouldn't let me. How am I? I mean, how's Larissa?"

Evelyn rolled her eyes. "Whiny. Sullen. Keeps saying she's sick of this dream and wants to wake up."

"Did the Benadryl work?"

"For a little while."

"Give her more," I said. "I'll pull out some more pills." From the corner of my eye, I could see a neighbor coming down the street. I slipped around the back of the house before he could wonder why a beautiful blond girl was standing on my front porch talking to herself. I let myself in the back door, Evelyn following soundlessly.

Upstairs, the door to my bedroom was open a crack. A girl lay on my bed crying. She was me but not me. No one really knows what she looks like to other people, but I've seen enough pictures and I've felt my face move. Her expressions were not mine. I couldn't imagine that anyone would ever believe she was me—but then, no one had questioned that I was her. Her hair was loose and greasy and falling in her face. She was still wearing the jeans and fake-layered top I'd fallen asleep in. They didn't look nearly as hot as I'd thought they did.

After putting a couple more Benadryl on the bathroom counter, I tiptoed back down the stairs, my breathing coming fast.

"Well?" Evelyn asked.

I pictured myself upstairs. "Are my shoulders really that big?"

She didn't answer, which I took as a yes.

I grabbed the pad and pen next to the phone.

Mom,
  Got a headache & went to bed. Please don't wake me up.
  See you in the morning.

       Love,
       Claire

I stared at the pad, surprised. Even though it came from Larissa's hand, the handwriting was my own, upright and plain.

Next up: stalling my mother. I called the clinic and took a deep breath. "This is Marjorie Humphrey—Mary Humphrey's daughter? I know it's late, but my mother is complaining of chest pains and really needs to see Dr. Martin." I sounded appropriately panicked—not difficult to do at this point.

And then: "Yes, I know she should go to the emergency room, but she refuses. And if I call nine-one-one, she'll lock herself in her bedroom."

Mary Humphrey has been my mother's patient since before I was born. She has medical "emergencies" at least twice a month and has said she'd rather die in bed than go to the hospital. If my mother had still been at the clinic, she would have waited hours for Mary Humphrey. But my mother had already left.

Next, I tried her cell phone, trying to remember which patients she had (foolishly) given the number to. But when her voice mail picked up, I disconnected.

"My mother's on her way home!" I told Evelyn. "Tell Larissa to take that Benadryl—now!"

My mother was pulling into the driveway just as I rounded the side of my house.

"Hello." She smiled, obviously assuming I was a friend of her daughter's.

"Hi." I blinked nervously, believing for an instant that my mother would know me, that she would look into Larissa's eyes and see my soul.

"I'm Dr. Martin," she said. "And you're . . . ?"

"Larissa. I'm staying nearby. Babysitting for the summer. I met Claire on the beach." I tried to think of more to say—anything to keep her out of that house—but my head was buzzing from fear and nothing would come.

"Is Claire home?"

I nodded. "But she has a headache, so she went to bed."

My mother frowned with concern. "I'd better go check on her then."

"No!"

She looked at me. I swallowed. "I mean—well, she said she just wanted to be alone. To sleep. I don't think you should wake her up."

My mother began to move toward the door with purpose.

"Wait!" I said.

She looked at me. I tried to think of a way to stall her, ingeniously blinking, clearing my throat, and saying "um" several times. That killed at least four seconds.

She rose her eyebrows as if to say, "Well?"

My eyes fell on the lavender plants that lined the front walk. In the spring they were covered with bees.

"Ouch!" I yelped, grabbing my skinny arm.

"What's wrong?"

"Ohhhh!" I moaned. "Owww!"

"What is it?" She hurried toward me.

"Bee sting!" I gasped.

"You want me to get you some ice?"

I shook my head. "I'm allergic!"

"Do you have an EpiPen?" she asked, as I'd known she would.

97

I shook my head. "Forgot it. Lost it." I began to whimper.

"It's okay," she said calmly. "I'm a doctor. I can take you to my clinic, give you a shot."

I nodded, speechless with relief: Sometimes my mother carried a spare EpiPen in her car or her purse, in which case I was fully prepared to transition into a fake asthma attack.

"I'll just tell my daughter where we're going," she said.

"No!" I clutched my neck. "It's getting hard to breathe," I said in a strangled voice. Forget the swim team: I should try out for the school play.

I should have gone with the asthma attack, I thought as, fifteen minutes later, my mother jabbed a needle into my fat-free thigh. An asthma attack would have meant a nice little breathing treatment. A shot of epinephrine was going to make me feel like I'd just downed five cups of coffee. Plus, that needle really hurt.

"Do you want to call your parents?" my mother asked.

I shifted my weight on the examining table and shook my head. "Mom's on a cruise. Dad's—" Oh, crap, where was Dad anyway? "I'm not allowed to talk to Dad until October."

She nodded without surprise. "Is there any adult I can call? Normally, I'd need an adult's permission to treat you, but of course there wasn't time."

"I'm just babysitting." I pictured Mrs. Sealy. "But I don't think anyone has any kind of legal control over me. Just my mom, and she's not around."

My mother nodded, considering. "Well, I need to make up a report about you, at least." She logged on to the computer (every exam room has one) and hit a few keys. "We create a file for anyone who comes through here."

She filled in my name. (Fortunately, I'd seen Larissa's last name, Hughes, on those envelopes in her dresser.) When I told her my birth date—keeping my voice as casual as possible—she exclaimed, "You and Claire were born on the same day!"

"Really?" I said. "Wow. I guess it explains why we were, you know. Drawn to each other."

She needed my weight for her records. I stepped on the scale and said, "Whoa!" when the number came up.

"Are you always this thin?" she asked gently.

"Oh, no," I said as if that were an absurd idea (which for me it is). "I had this really bad stomach bug a couple of weeks ago? I guess I dropped more weight than I realized."

She wanted to call Mrs. Sealy, but when I swore for the third time that I didn't know her phone number (I really didn't), she called the rental company for the house information. The rental company was closed, so she called the real-estate agent at home. The real-estate agent has been coming to my mother for years. The real-estate agent suffers from hypertension and kidney stones.

Consuela answered the phone. Mrs. Sealy wasn't home yet, she told my mother. Consuela was unimpressed with my brush with death.

My mother drove me back to the Ice Cube House. I checked the clock on her dashboard: It was almost eight o'clock.

"Won't you come in?" I asked, honestly hoping she'd say yes. It wasn't just that I wanted to keep her away from our house as long as possible. My mother was the first person who

99

had been kind to me since I'd become Larissa. Well, besides Nate, anyway.

"Thanks, but I need to get home to Claire." Claire. If she had taken the Benadryl, she should be fast asleep by now. My mother scribbled something on a piece of paper. "This is my home number. Call me if you have any more problems. You have the extra EpiPen and the prescription I gave you?"

I nodded.

She squeezed my hand and held my eyes. "Good luck, Larissa. Take care of yourself."

Oddly, I felt my eyes fill with tears. My mother was sitting right next to me, but I missed her terribly. All these years, I'd suspected that she cared more about her patients than she did about me. But now I saw the way she looked at Larissa, with care and concern and a thousand good intentions. I wanted desperately to see love in her eyes. I now realized that she looked at only one person that way: me.

I blinked twice and said good-bye. My mother waited until I'd disappeared into the blocky white house, and then she drove home to her sleeping daughter.

16

CAMERON AND PRESCOTT WERE IN BED, fast asleep. Consuela was gone—probably off at the store buying eye of newt or a flying broom. Mrs. Sealy was home, as perhaps she had been when my mother had called, sitting out on the deck with a glass of white wine, staring at the ocean.

I pulled open the slider and stepped out onto the deck. The air was tingly with cold; a fog was rolling in. The sky was that purplish black color it gets just after sunset. Below us, the waves crashed and pulled back in a soothing, endless rhythm.

"I'm back," I said.

Mrs. Sealy turned her head and nodded. Her eyes looked oddly distant. "Everything okay?" she asked.

"Yes." I was sure she'd ask me where I'd been, why I'd left her boys again.

"I didn't know you were allergic to bees," she said instead.

"Neither did I."

I waited for her to say something else, to express anger or concern: something, anything.

The waves crashed. The moon reflected a long white pathway on the ocean, as if beckoning us to follow.

"I think I'll go to bed," I announced.

Mrs. Sealy didn't respond.

All I wanted was to sleep and drift back to my own body, my own life, but the epinephrine shot left me feeling jittery. After lying in the dark for a half hour, my pulse racing in my ears, I finally turned on the light. There wasn't much to do in this room—no books, no television, no computer—but I didn't want to go into the main room and risk running into Mrs. Sealy.

I opened the top dresser drawer and pulled out Larissa's letters. There was the birthday card from her father, plus some envelopes. The top envelope just said "Krystal" where the full return address ought to be. I opened it up and slipped out yet another birthday card.

> *Lari,*
>   *I know you hate me but you're still my friend*
> *and we'll be friends forever, all right? Forget what*
> *Bella said, she's just jealous, but she's funny,*
> *that's why I like her. I'm sorry about the mean*
> *things I said about you, it was just me and Bella*
> *kidding around. You know that, right? Can't wait*

till school is over and we can get out of this place.
I hate it.

But anyway I just wanted to say happy
birthday, babe!

Love ya,
Krystal

Wow. Even someone who looked like Larissa can get stuck with a backstabbing friend like Avon. The difference between us was that Larissa still liked Krystal enough to keep her card and take it on vacation with her.

Suddenly I missed Beanie. I hope she wasn't too mad that I hadn't shown up at the beach today.

There were several other simple, white business envelopes addressed to Larissa in care of Krystal. *Why not just send them to her home address?* I wondered. As soon as I thought about it, though, I knew: they were letters from her father.

My Girl,

Do you remember when you were little and we
used to play Three Wishes? Well, if I had three
wishes now, I would choose these:

That I could see you every morning.
That I could see you every night.
That you would never be sad again.

All my love,
Daddy

And the next letter:

> My Girl,
>
> I would be lying if I said I wasn't angry at your
> mother, but I don't want you to be angry too.
> Anger will only make you feel sad. When you were
> a baby my favorite thing was to make you laugh. It
> wasn't hard. Now it seems like you hardly ever
> laugh anymore. It breaks my heart to think it is at
> least partly my fault.
>
> Your mother and I both love you, and we both
> want to spend as much time with you as we can. I
> will see you in October. Until then, know that you
> are always in my thoughts and my dreams. I love
> you, my girl.
>
> Daddy

And the most recent letter, dated a couple of weeks earlier:

> Dearest Larissa,
>
> You know that I would drop everything and
> come see you if I could, but you've got to stop
> calling me. I am so afraid that your mother will find
> out about our talks and make it even harder for us
> to see each other. We have to do what the lawyers
> say, no matter how much we hate it. Please, baby,
> don't risk losing our October visit. It's the only thing
> that keeps me going these days.

I have so many regrets, Larissa, I don't even know where to start. I am sorry I walked out on your mother (even though she told me to go) because it's the thing she can bring up to the lawyers, again and again. I am sorry I missed those alimony payments early on. Mostly, I am sorry I gave your mother full custody. I really thought it would be best for you, not having to change houses all the time, especially since my apartment isn't very nice.

The one thing I am not sorry about, the one thing in my life I did right, is you. It is because your mother and I both love you so much that we don't want to share.

When we see each other in October, we can talk about going back to court to see if we can have weekly visitations. Or maybe your mother and I can share custody. I could move closer to your mother's house so you wouldn't be too far from school.

Until then, my girl, enjoy your summer with your mom, and know your daddy loves you.

When I finished reading, I tucked the letters back into their envelopes and placed them back in the drawer. My hands were trembling, whether from the epinephrine or from rage, I didn't know.

My whole life I had dreamed of having a father, of knowing a father. Larissa had a father who loved her, who'd do anything for her, and she wasn't allowed to see him. Larissa could have been with her father right now, rather than in this cold and hateful house. Her mother didn't even want to be with her—but she wouldn't let Larissa's father have his way.

I rummaged around the drawer some more and came up with a makeup bag and a cell phone. I turned the phone on and checked the address list: Mom, Dad, Krystal, and several boys (one of whom she had labeled, simply, "Stud"). All in all, it was a pretty short list. I checked for messages: none. *Stupid Krystal,* I thought. *She's probably out with stupid Bella making fun of Larissa while poor Larissa is stuck here in this concrete house with no one to talk to, not even a cat.*

I heard footsteps over my head: Mrs. Sealy was walking up the stairs on her way to her bedroom. The door closed, and then it was quiet.

What was Mr. Sealy like? I wondered. If there was anything to that whole "opposites attract" thing, maybe he was the nice parent, an ice-cream-buying, soccer-coaching kind of dad. Then again, maybe not. Since he wasn't due for two more days, it didn't look like I'd find out.

I sat on the edge of the bed, staring at the clock. It was 9:30. The epinephrine had partly worn off, but I still felt wired. Sleep was out of the question, for a couple of hours at least. Why not make the most of my babe-a-licious looks?

I waited ten minutes and then opened my door a crack. The house was dark. I slipped on tight, faded jeans, a strappy pink shirt over a lacy pink bra, a brown sweater hoodie, and the pink flip-flops I loved, the ones with the sunset-colored flowers. I hadn't worn this much pink since I was five. I thought of my clothes at home and couldn't come up with a single item of pink clothing. Maybe I'd try on a pink T-shirt the next time my mother and I went to the mall. Maybe it wouldn't look as ridiculous on me as I'd always assumed it would.

I grabbed a brush and stroked my long blond hair to make it fluffy. I was about to pull out the makeup bag when I looked in the mirror. Larissa's beauty surprised me every time. My face was rosy from the day in the sun. My eyelashes were naturally dark, my lips plump. I wondered why Larissa even bothered buying makeup. She was already perfect.

I shoved a couple of pillows under my covers to make it look like a sleeping body and turned out the light. Flip-flops in hand, I crept down the hall, the floor chilly on my feet. When I reached the sliding glass door, I took a deep breath and opened it as quietly as I could. The noise echoed off the hard surfaces. I froze for an instant but heard nothing from inside the house. The ocean drowned out the sound of my movements. I slid the door shut behind me.

I scurried to the side of the house, hiding in the shadows as I crossed the lawn. The night had grown murky; clouds covered the moon. From the edge of the lawn, I sprinted for the concrete stairs that led down the rock wall to the beach and tiptoed down as fast as I could without slipping.

A wave splashed my toes almost immediately. It was high tide.

I headed along the damp sand toward the public beach. My heart raced with fear. There was no one around, so what was I afraid of? That a sea monster would jump out of the black ocean and pull me into the water?

Another wave rolled in, reaching all the way to the rocks and soaking the hems of my jeans. Lights twinkled far out on the horizon: fishing boats, maybe.

When I reached the public beach, I trudged up to the drier sand. It stuck to my wet feet. Normally, I love the feel of the cold beach on my feet at night. It surprises me with every step. Tonight it just made me move faster, toward the people, the fire, the warmth. I slipped on the flip-flops to protect Larissa's tender feet from broken shells.

The first person I saw was this girl I knew from swim team. She was a year older than I was, tall, with frizzy brown hair. She was loud and funny and I liked her.

"Hi!" I said, approaching her with an odd sense of relief and forgetting for an instant who I was—or who I looked like, at any rate.

She gawked at me. I expected her to smile, to say hello. But she didn't. She just stared. And then her eyes narrowed and she looked away.

"Sorry, I thought you were someone else," I said, thinking, *See if I ever talk to you again.*

There was a bunch of people near the bonfire. It was hard to tell just how many in the dim light, but I'd say at least thirty, maybe more. Most kids were wearing hoodie sweatshirts and jeans. A few were still in their bathing suits, though I couldn't imagine how they could stand the cold. Kids drank from Coke cans and Sprite bottles. The smell of beer mingled with smoke and ocean while shouts and laughter mixed with the roar of the waves.

A couple of people stared at me. I saw Ricki and Dayna sitting by the fire. (They knew about the bonfires and I didn't?) I avoided their eyes and scanned the crowd. Where was Nate? I walked away from the bonfire and saw a couple pressed against each other, kissing. The cloud passed away from the moon, lighting the scene enough for me to recognize them.

"No way!" I said without thinking.

Ryan and Avon turned their heads to look at me. When Ryan recognized me, his eyes widened and he stepped away from Avon. She put a hand on his arm as if to claim him as her property.

I can't wait to tell Beanie, I thought reflexively.

"Were you looking for me?" Ryan asked.

I looked from him to Avon. My mouth twitched. I tossed my tangled blond hair out of my face. "Does it matter? It looks like you're pretty busy."

Ryan took another step away from Avon and jerked his arm to release her grip. He shoved his hands into his jeans. "This doesn't mean anything. We were just playing around."

Avon made a funny mewing sound and slapped his face. It sounded like a wave hitting the side of a boat. He covered his cheek with his hand and looked at her, confused. She shot me a look of horror and hatred and ran off toward the bonfire.

Ryan seemed to forget about her immediately. He stared at me. All of this staring was getting on my nerves. "You wanna go somewhere?" he asked finally.

My mouth dropped open. After an instant, I felt something

bubbling up inside of me until finally I laughed: a mean, nasal sound. "Dream on, Burger Boy." I ran a hand through my masses of blond hair and flashed a cruel, dazzling smile before turning my back on him and striding away.

I wasn't scared anymore. It was as if my nastiness had given me some kind of strange power: Nothing could hurt me. *Could Larissa have left some part of herself behind?* I wondered.

Near the bonfire, Avon sat huddled with Ricki and Dayna. Ricki glared at me. A surge of pity for Avon hit me, but I got over it. There were plenty of familiar faces around the bonfire, but still no Nate. Giving up, I turned to walk back to the Ice Cube House and almost ran into him.

He blinked at me and then smiled. I smiled back. This time, I didn't mind being stared at.

"You're here," he said. He wore faded jeans, his blue "Sandyland Swimming" sweatshirt, and an enormous grin.

We smiled at each other with a silence that should have been awkward but wasn't.

"Do you guys do this much?" I asked. "The bonfires, I mean."

He shrugged. "Every week or two."

I nodded, feeling a stab of pain at having never been invited.

"Let's get away from here," I said. "We can go farther down the beach."

I knew everybody was watching us, but I didn't care. It's not like there was anything much to see: just the most beautiful girl in the world walking down the beach with the most beautiful boy in the world. The Golden Couple. We were such a perfect match, I felt like it deserved a comment, like, "We'd look good together on a shopping bag or a billboard. Or maybe on a bottle of cologne."

But I didn't say any of that because I didn't want him to think I was, you know. Vain.

After a bit, the bonfire became a distant glow, and we plopped down on the chilly sand.

"You cold?" Nate asked. "You can borrow my sweatshirt."

I shook my head. "I like the beach at night. Being cold is part of it."

He gazed at the dark ocean. "You know when I like the beach best?"

Somehow I knew the answer. "January?"

He turned his head to look at me. "How did you know?"

I pictured the winter light, the vast, open sand. "It's my favorite time on the beach too. It's so empty that I can pretend that I own it. Or, even better, that no one owns anything because there's no one here. Sometimes I look around and imagine what it was like when it was just the Indians here, living off the land."

"You've been here in the winter?"

Oops. "Here? No. But other beaches. For weekends and stuff." (Nice save.)

Satisfied with my answer, he returned his gaze to the ocean. "What do you think the Indians ate?" he mused. "Just fish and berries?"

"Nah—I bet they ordered breakfast burritos and milk shakes from the snack shack."

He laughed and turned to me. "You're funny."

111

"That surprises you."

"Not really." He didn't sound very convincing.

"I'm more than just a pretty face." I tossed my hair for dramatic effect.

"I know you are. I've known that since . . ."

"When?" I asked, a little too eagerly.

He shot me a sly grin. "Since the first time I saw you."

"Oh." I swallowed with disappointment.

He touched my face. "What?"

"Nothing." I picked up some sand and let it run through my fingers. "Just, the first time you saw me . . . "

"It blew me away. How pretty you were."

I tried to smile.

"*Pretty* isn't the right word," he said, mistaking my lukewarm reaction as a desire for greater praise. "You're, like, a goddess. I've never seen anyone even half as beautiful as you. I mean, not in real life, anyway. There's girls on television and stuff, but they've got all that makeup and hair extensions. And they do stuff with lighting to make them look better. Those girls could be three hundred pounds, with hook noses, and they'd still make them look good."

My Golden Couple glow had passed. I felt like he was talking about someone else—which of course, he was. I kept playing with the sand and didn't say anything.

"I should probably just shut up now," he said.

"Huh?" I looked up.

"The first time I saw you, I guess I acted like an idiot. And I didn't think you liked me at all. And you were so pretty, but I kind of thought you were, well, I don't want to say a bitch, but —" He stopped dead. "Oh, God. I've just blown it, haven't I?"

I burst out laughing. "No, not at all."

He took a deep breath. "There's something about you— some . . . something. When I saw you at the beach today, I thought you'd blow me off again, so I wasn't going to say anything. But then, just seeing how cool you were with those kids— and how hard you tried in the water, even after you got knocked over. I mean, you're just . . . fearless. And so, yeah, at first I *did* think you were just a pretty face. But you're more than that. A lot more."

He fell back on the sand, crossing his arms under his head. "I'm not good at this."

I lay down next to him, crossing my arms as he had done. Our elbows touched. "Maybe you just need practice. You can keep talking, if you want. I mean, about how fabulous I am."

He laughed. "Nah. I wouldn't want to use up all of my good material at once. Hey! Did you see that?"

"What?"

"A shooting star! Make a wish! Look—there's another one!"

"Nate?"

"Yeah?"

"That's an airplane. It just went behind a cloud."

Silence, and then: "Oh, crap." We smiled in the darkness.

"What did you wish?" I asked.

"If I tell you, it won't come true."

"It won't come true anyway," I said. "You can't wish on an airplane."

"I can if I want to."

I thought it about it a moment and then said, "Good point. In that case, I think I'll wish on the airplane too."

Later we held hands as he walked me home. The water splashed our feet. I took off the flip-flops so the flowers wouldn't get ruined. My toes were numb, and my sandy cuffs chafed my ankles. I didn't care. Our pace was slow, but eventually we reached the rocks that kept the ocean from washing away the Ice Cube House.

Nate took my other hand, the one holding what I thought was both my flip-flops, and we faced each other. "You lost a shoe," he said.

He was right. I was down to one pink flip-flop. The other was probably on its way out to sea.

"Oh, no." I felt worse than I should have over the loss of something plastic and rubber.

"I can go back and look for it."

I shook my head. "I won't need it after tonight."

He pulled me over to the rock wall, and we scrambled onto a boulder right next to the "Keep Off Rocks" sign. The moon had risen high in the sky, escaping the clouds and giving the ocean an eerie glow. He put his arm around me. I leaned against his chest, my long blond hair cascading over his sweat-shirt. The water flowed toward us and then back, forward and back, in an endless, unstoppable rhythm, like the beating of a heart.

"Is it nice staying in that place?" he asked, looking above the rocks.

"Not as nice as you'd expect. It's . . . cold. Everything's white and steel. Most of the floors are concrete." Then I thought about Larissa's body. "But it does have certain benefits."

He stroked my head. I leaned into his hand like a cat. "Do you really have to leave tomorrow?" he murmured.

I nodded. "I wish I could stay." It was true—I did. For a little bit longer, at least. But then, school was starting tomorrow, and there was no way I could miss it.

"Maybe you'll come back next summer."

"Maybe." I looked in his light eyes, and in that moment I believed he was seeing me—the real me, not the me in Larissa's body or even the me in my own body, but the very essence of myself.

Then he put his hand on the back of my head and we kissed and I forgot all about whose body I was in. It was just me, Nate's lips, and the pounding of the waves. I slipped my arms around him and held on tight. He tasted salty. It wasn't until later that I wondered whether this counted as my first kiss. Did I have to use my own lips?

"I should get going," he said finally. "I was supposed to be home over an hour ago. School starts tomorrow."

"What time is it?"

He checked his watch. "Almost midnight."

"Midnight?" I gasped. "I've got to go."

We slid down the rocks and stood for one last moment on the cold sand, holding hands and looking at each other as if we could stop time.

But we couldn't. I kissed him on the cheek and whispered, "Good-bye. I'll never forget you." Then I scurried up the stairs without letting myself look back. I fled through the shadows at the side of the house, dropping the single pink flip-flop into a trash can before sliding open the glass door.

The house was dark and quiet. My pillows were just where I'd left them, made into the bed to look like my body. Well, like Larissa's body. I'd need more pillows to make it look like mine.

The big gray T-shirt was dirty from the beach, so I stripped down to my pink underwear and crawled under the covers, shoving the pillows back up where they belonged. It was a minute before midnight.

I closed my eyes and thought of Nate. "Good night, sweet prince," I whispered as I fell into a deep and heavy sleep.

17

"Boo!" The voice was loud, close.

I'm dreaming, I thought. *I must be dreaming.*

"Boo!"

I kept my eyes squeezed shut, trying to remember my earlier dream. Something about Nate. About kissing Nate.

"BOO!" This wasn't a dream. Someone was yelling in my ear. Only they weren't actually saying "Boo," they were saying:

"BOOB!"

My eyes popped open. It was morning, the gray light filtering through Larissa's pathetic excuse for a window. Prescott stood next to me, level with my face. I'd pushed my sheets off in the night, exposing the lacy little pink bra and my—

"BOOBS!"

"Be quiet!" I sat up and grabbed the sheet in one motion, pulling it up to cover me. I looked around the room in amazement. What was I still doing here? What had gone wrong? Where was Larissa?

Prescott clutched his stomach and bent over laughing. Prescott's cackling was even more annoying than Cameron's whining. "I saw your boobies! I saw your boobies!"

"SHUT UP!" I said, thinking, *If you were a dog, someone would put you down.*

He stared at me, shocked, and then he dissolved into angry tears. "You can't say shut up! I'm gonna tell!" He was wearing short summer pajamas, pale blue with airplanes. His blond hair was sticking up on one side.

"Fine," I snapped. "Tell away."

"You're gonna be in trouble! My mom's not gonna let you babysit us anymore."

"Really? That's wonderful. I should have told you to shut up a long time ago." Seriously—it wasn't a bad strategy.

At that, he crumpled to his feet and began pounding the floor. "I hate you! I hate you! I hate you!"

I closed my eyes, my jaw tense. "And I'm supposed to care?"

His howls turned to whimpers. "You don't like me." He sniffled.

I was just about to say, "Yes, that's right. I don't like you, and I don't like your brother or your mother either," but then I caught a look at his face and it stopped me. For the first time since I'd been here, Prescott didn't look like the devil. Instead, he just looked like a sad and lonely four-year-old boy. (Of course, I reasoned, given that I'm a body switcher, it's entirely possible that Prescott is a shape changer.)

I took a deep breath. "I like you."

"No, you don't."

"I do. I like you. You're : . ." Here I struggled to come up with something positive. "You're tough," I said finally. He was too: tough and feisty.

He sat up and wiped his tears with the back of his bunched-up first. "Do you really think so?"

Still holding the sheet over my front, I used the other hand to reach for a tissue on my nightstand. I handed it to Prescott. "Oh, yeah. You're one tough dude all right. The toughest four-year-old I've ever seen."

"Larissa?"

"Yeah."

He held out the tissue. "Can you help me blow?"

Cameron got up soon after Prescott. I stirred their chocolate milk as I watched the clock, counting the minutes until school began. Had my mother discovered the new me? Had Larissa figured out that this wasn't just a dream?

I was so agitated, I could barely sit still. When Mrs. Sealy finally appeared, in yoga clothes again, I blurted out, "Can I go for a walk?"

Mrs. Sealy fluttered her eyelashes tensely before saying, "Consuela will be out running errands this morning. I need you to be extra helpful, Larissa."

I nodded silently while Prescott, to my amazement, took my hand.

My waffles were way better than Consuela's, but Mrs. Sealy didn't have any because she was "avoiding glutens." Instead she drank some nasty-looking green stuff that she said was "cleansing." She offered me some. I passed. The boys had two waffles each. I put away four, even though my stomach started to hurt after three. I knew it was wrong to beef up Larissa, but it was the only thing giving me any pleasure right now.

After breakfast, Mrs. Sealy slathered the boys' pink skin with sunblock. "While I'm at yoga, you can take the boys down to the beach for an hour or two. Before the sun gets strong. After you've finished the breakfast dishes, I mean."

I wore the brown bikini under shorts and a T-shirt, not that it mattered. I didn't plan to spend much time at the beach anyway. I stuck Larissa's cell phone in my pocket, though I couldn't imagine who I'd call.

I expected to find Evelyn sitting on my front step. When I didn't see her there, I led the boys around to the back and peered through a window into the empty kitchen. "I have a friend who lives here," I explained. "I thought she might be home."

I was seriously tempted to let myself into the house using the spare key that we kept in a bird feeder, but I was afraid that Cameron would rat me out to his mother. That kid was a total suck-up.

I sat on the back steps. "Well. I guess she's not here." My voice quavered. I thought about my mother. Had she taken me—that is, the girl who looks like me—to the emergency room? To a mental hospital?

I pulled out Larissa's cell phone and dialed the medical clinic. "Is Dr. Martin in today?"

She was.

"And is she . . . there all day?"

She would be.

I closed the phone and exhaled with relief. If my mother was at work, then she hadn't discovered me missing yet. Was I missing?

"Let's go to the beach," I said to the boys, who were doing their best to destroy my mother's herb garden.

Nate wasn't at the beach, of course. No one between the ages of five and eighteen was there. They were all in school.

"When do you start school?" I asked Cameron as he filled a red plastic mold with sand. The mold was shaped like a car. He shrugged. He turned the mold over. The sand fell out, loose.

"Are you going into kindergarten?" I asked.

His face turned red. Well, redder. "I'm in preschool! My dad said I can't go to kindergarten yet because they don't let crybabies go to kindergarten!" At that, he started to cry.

"You're not a crybaby," I said.

"You mean it?"

"I mean it." I took his shovel and dug until I reached damp sand. "Here. Let's fill the mold again. I bet it'll work this time."

When the sun broke through the fog, we headed back to the rock wall. I climbed the concrete steps to the Ice Cube House ahead of the boys, who were studying some barnacles on the boulders. At the top of the steps, a brand-new boogie board lay on the grass. I started to reach for it when I noticed someone out of the corner of my eye.

There was a man standing by the downstairs slider. When he saw me, he emerged from the shadows and walked in my direction. He was middle aged, his blond hair streaked with gray. He wore a black polo shirt and khaki pants. He looked respectable enough, but he scared me. There was something hard about his squinty blue eyes.

Ever since my encounter with the tattooed jogger, I'd been skittish around strange men.

"Can I help you?" I asked, my heart beating faster.

"I would hope so, Larissa," he said, glaring at me.

I blinked in confusion. I didn't know what to say.

"Perhaps you can tell me where I can find my wife and children?" he said finally.

At that, I heard a little voice behind me call out, "Daddy!" Prescott darted across the lawn and grabbed his father's legs.

"Hey there, Sport!" Mr. Sealy reached down to pick up Prescott, then tossed him in the air. I tried not to gasp as Prescott's solid but small body flew above his father's head and was relieved when he was safely back on the ground.

I looked back at the steps to make sure that Cameron hadn't been washed away by a rogue wave. He stood there, the ocean behind him, looking very shy and small, even though he was older and taller than his brother.

Mr. Sealy slapped his hands together as if wiping off traces of Prescott. "Hello, Cameron."

"Hi, Daddy."

"Are you just planning to stand there, or are you going to come over to say hello?"

Cameron skulked across the lawn. When he reached his father, he held out his right hand, and they shook like two businessmen sealing a deal.

122

Mr. Sealy peered down at Cameron with his icy blue eyes. "You want me to throw you in the air?"

Cameron shook his head and wrapped his skinny arms around his concave chest.

Mr. Sealy rolled his eyes and then turned his gaze to me. I had been holding my breath, I suddenly realized, gulping some air.

"Where is Mrs. Sealy?" he asked.

"Yoga, I think."

Consuela had lunch waiting: peanut-butter-and-jelly sandwiches for the kids, chicken salad for the adults.

"You eating?" she asked me, eyebrows raised.

"Oh, yeah."

"You want your chicken salad plain or you want it on a croissant?"

"You got croissants? Awesome."

And then the most amazing thing happened. Consuela smiled.

Consuela carried a tray with the Sealys' lunches to the outdoor teak table. She set their places and put up the umbrella. She had already put out two pitchers: one of iced tea, the other of chocolate milk.

The ocean was a brilliant blue, the seagull calls like mermaid music. Beyond the breakers, a seal popped its head out and then dove back into the depths. It was like a setting out of a magazine, and for a moment I forgot that I was supposed to be eating my lunch in Sandyland High's boxy cafeteria with the acoustic tiles and a view of the parking lot.

I could get used to this.

I helped the boys scoot their big wooden chairs closer to the table. They were at eye level to their lunches, but they knew better than to complain. Mr. Sealy held a newspaper with one hand, his fork with the other. I got my square plate from the kitchen. Consuela had put a slice of cantaloupe next to my chicken salad sandwich. I turned to smile at her, but she was busy cleaning the kitchen and ignored me.

When I stepped out onto the deck, I breathed the ocean air and held it in my lungs for a moment before letting it out in a calming, salty exhalation. Plate in hand, I took a couple of steps toward the table. Mr. Sealy looked up from his reading.

"Larissa?"

"Yes?"

"If you don't mind, I'd rather make this a family lunch. You can eat in the kitchen. With Connie."

I stopped dead. "Right." I headed back into the house. Mr. Sealy went back to his paper.

Inside, Consuela was wiping down the big stainless-steel table. I just stood there for a moment, feeling like a kid who doesn't know where to sit in the cafeteria. Who was Beanie eating with? I wondered. I'd have given anything to be able to stick a plastic cafeteria tray next to hers.

Consuela stopped wiping for a moment and looked up at me. "You sit. Is okay."

I placed my plate down carefully and slipped into a chair. Consuela looked out at Mr. Sealy and muttered some words that they didn't teach in high school Spanish.

"Have you worked for the Sealys long?" I asked.

"Huh?" She went back to wiping. "Seven months."

"Do you . . . like it?"

She looked at me as if I'd just said something ridiculous. "Is a job."

"Oh." There was nothing else to say.

Mrs. Sealy came bursting in just as I was finishing my sandwich. She dropped her keys on the counter and looked around the room. "Is my husband here? He left a message on my cell phone."

She spotted him on the deck. "Darling!" She pushed open the screen door. "What a wonderful surprise. I didn't think you were coming until tomorrow."

"I told you I might come this morning to avoid the weekend traffic. You need to listen." He stood up and they kissed on the cheek like two people who didn't know each other very well but wanted to pretend they liked each other.

Mrs. Sealy gave the boys the biggest hugs I'd seen yet and let Cameron crawl in her lap.

Consuela brought Mrs. Sealy a plain boneless chicken breast, some cantaloupe, and a glass of wine. She refilled Mr. Sealy's glass with iced tea and then came back inside, where she pretended to work but was obviously spying. I chewed my sandwich as slowly as I could manage and sat back to listen to their conversation.

"Isn't it a bit early?" Mr. Sealy asked, nodding at the wine.

Mrs. Sealy squinted at the ocean. "I'm on vacation."

"The house is a monstrosity," her husband remarked without much emotion.

"I like it. It's restful."

"Who knew restfulness would cost so much money?"

"It's only for two weeks. And it's been a really special bonding time for me and the boys."

I waited until they had finished eating to go back out onto the deck. "Excuse me?" I asked timidly, my back pressed against the screen. "Would it be okay if I went for a walk?"

Mrs. Sealy said, "Larissa, I don't think that—" when Mr. Sealy cut her off.

"I think we can handle our own children for one afternoon," he said.

Mrs. Sealy sat frozen for a moment. "It's just that I told Suzanne I would keep an eye on her," she murmured.

Suzanne was Larissa's mother, I guessed.

"What kind of trouble can she possibly get into around here? This town is dead." Mr. Sealy didn't bother lowering his voice. It was like I wasn't even there or maybe just like I didn't matter. He picked up his newspaper. "We should have gone to Mexico, like I said."

"Do you know when my school year starts?" I blurted out— even though the real Larissa wouldn't need to ask.

"Tuesday, I think," Mrs. Sealy said, looking up from the ground. "The day after Labor Day. Don't you know? Your mother said it was no big deal missing it—they don't teach much in the first week, anyway. She said it would be nicer for you to have a week at the beach."

"Nicer?" I said. "Oh, yeah—that's why she sent me here. Not so she could, say, go on a cruise with her boyfriend. Or so you could have a free babysitter."

My words surprised me as much as anyone else. I had never spoken that way to an adult. But there was a freedom, a power, in knowing I'd escape any punishment.

Mrs. Sealy and I stared at each other—a face-off—until Prescott said, "Ooooh, Larissa, you're gonna get in trouble."

And this was the kid I'd called tough. Little weenie.

Mr. Sealy didn't care what I said. He just wanted to get rid of me so he could go back to his paper. "Enjoy your walk," he said coldly.

"I plan to."

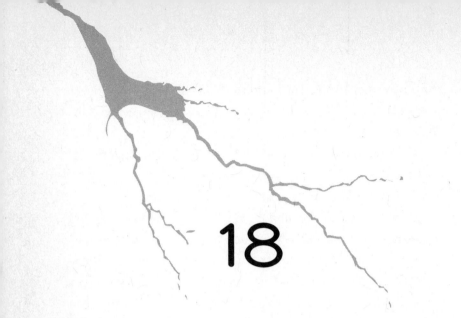

18

MY LITTLE BLUE HOUSE WAS QUIET: no ghosts on the front stoop, even. The mail carrier was driving down the street in her jeep, pulling over to stuff boxes. I resisted the urge to say hello, strolling around the block instead. When I came back, she was gone.

I went to the front door, rang the bell, and shouted hello a couple of times. This was for effect. If anyone saw me, I could say I tried the front door first before going around back to look for my new BFF Claire.

The key was in the birdhouse that I'd made in fifth grade, its rainbow paint faded from years in the sun. I took it off the low branch and tilted it until the key slid to the front opening. I dug the key out with my index finger, leaving a line of black underneath my nail. Damn. I was totally going to need a new manicure.

The house was empty. I sensed that the moment I walked inside, but I went upstairs anyway. There were my books, my pictures, my computer. There was my bed, neatly made, Fluffernutter sprawled in the middle. When he saw me, he darted out of the room and across the hall.

I followed him into my mother's room. "Fluff, it's me!" I peeked under the bed. His yellow eyes glowed. He didn't blink.

"Come here, you furball!"

He stayed put. So much for that secret sixth sense that animals are supposed to have.

I turned on my computer and checked my e-mail. One friend had written to ask about my class schedule. Another had asked about swim-team trials. They were tomorrow. Missing the first day of school was bad enough, but I had to be back to my old self by tomorrow. I just *had* to.

There was one message from Beanie, which read, simply,

WHERE WERE YOU???????

I wrote back:

I am so sorry. I have not been myself the last couple of days. I will make it up to you.

I hit "send" before it occurred to me that Beanie might check the time of my reply—and I was supposed to be in school right now.

Was I in school right now? The thought freaked me out. Evelyn knew my sophomore year started today. Maybe she had convinced Larissa to go, had told her that this was just a continuation of her seemingly endless dream, like that one in which you're trying to open the door to a strange house but the key doesn't fit. Or that dream in which you're falling from a cliff but you never hit the ground. Or that dream in which you realize you're no longer willowy and beautiful but just some regular girl named Claire.

If I hurried, I could make it to school before the last bell. My bike was in the garage. As a precaution, as I rode down the driveway, I called out, "Thanks for letting me borrow your bike, Claire!"

As I rode, my heart raced for a bunch of reasons: Larissa was totally out of shape; it wigged me out to think that Larissa may have gone to school in my body; and two guys—men!—whistled at me and one car honked.

By the time I got to Sandyland High, I was so winded, sweaty, and shaky that I wondered how I'd ever get my bike back home.

I heard myself before I saw myself. I was walking along the side of the school, near the Dumpsters, when I heard myself laugh. My laugh sounds just like my mother's. Yup, I got my mother's lank hair, murky eyes, powerhouse build, and seal-pup laugh. Basically, I got everything from my mother except her knack for staying in her own body.

A girl who looked like me was leaning against the side of the brick building, partially hidden by the stinky brown Dumpsters, cigarette in hand. Instead of the new jeans and layered top, she wore my mother's short-sleeved black dress and black high-heeled shoes. There were five kids with her, two boys in long basketball shorts and oversize T-shirts and three girls decked out in tourniquet-tight jeans and the kinds of trampy, strappy shirts that are supposed to get you kicked out of school and maybe did.

"Claire?" I said carefully, Larissa's nasal voice vibrating in my ears.

She didn't notice me. Instead, she took a long drag on her cigarette and blew a smoke ring. The girl next to her had hair that was black and white in alternating streaks. She said, "Awesome, babe!" She tried to blow a smoke ring but failed.

I took a few steps closer. "Claire?" When again she didn't answer, I said, "*Larissa?*"—my voice louder than I had intended.

The kids all turned. The boys said hi. The girls glared.

The Claire-ish girl's eyes grew wide, and then she smiled. "Thanks for the smokes, Jessamine," she said to the girl with the zebra hair. She held up her cigarette-free hand in a wave. "Ciao, kids."

She pitched the cigarette onto the asphalt and ground it out with her foot. Then she strode toward me with a walk that was not my own, hips swaying, arms swinging. "Let's get some air," she said.

"We're already outside."

"Don't be so literal." She took my arm and, humming, led me to a sheltered corner.

Suddenly, I knew. "*Evelyn?*"

"Shh!" she said, her eyes darting around. "Don't blow my cover."

"You're supposed to be in math class."

"I know, but Beanie was in there, and I was afraid she'd know I wasn't you. I've been avoiding her all day, poor thing."

"Why didn't you just stay home?"

She sighed. "Your mother insisted on driving me to school, first day and all. She was really flattered when I asked to borrow her dress." She spun around once so I could admire it. "I thought you should wear something special, start the year off right. Bet your bottom dollar—after today, people are going to know who Claire Martin is!" She glanced back at the Dumpsters. "I'm actually having a pretty nice time. I've met some swell kids."

"You could have pretended to be sick."

"I don't like to lie. Besides, I was afraid of saying too much, of getting in trouble. I don't think we said ten words to each other all morning."

"Where's Larissa?"

"She's you know—around." She waved her hand in the air. "That nice girl Jessamine gave me the rest of her ciggies," she said as she pulled a pack of cigarettes from her bulky handbag, which I recognized as my mother's. "I promised myself I'd stop after just one, but smoking is so much better with real cigarettes—not to mention real lungs."

"Hey!" I grabbed the pack. "Those are *my* lungs!"

"You're right, sweetie." She batted her eyelashes in shame. "I shouldn't get you started on these nasty things. I just figured that a few cigarettes wouldn't make any"—she paused to cough—"difference."

"Time trials are tomorrow!" I tried to squish the cigarette pack in my hand and failed. Even Larissa's fingers were weak.

Evelyn reached into her purse—my mother's purse—and pulled out a compact. "Swim team, you mean? Well, let's hope you switch back tonight, because I've never been a big fan of the water." Evelyn had never shown much interest in my swimming, always encouraging me to try something more feminine, like figure skating or baton twirling. Yeah, like that was going to happen.

"Why didn't I switch back last night?" I asked. "I was asleep by midnight. And by the way, no one under sixty uses powder."

She flipped open the compact and patted her cheeks, chin, and nose. My nose.

"Larissa woke up around eleven and couldn't get back to sleep," Evelyn told me. "So we played Uno for probably an hour, though I'll tell you, it felt more like ten. She had to move all of the cards for the two of us, of course, which took all of the fun out of it. Assuming there was any fun in the first place."

"Uno?"

"She used to play it with her father. You know about her father?"

"Not much. Just that her parents are divorced and he doesn't get to see her much." I reached out and brushed some loose powder off of her cheek. I had to say, the powder looked better than I would have expected.

She dropped the compact in her bag and pulled out a lipstick. "Her father used to have a drinking problem. He's cleaned up his act—hasn't touched the stuff in years—but the courts are still making it really hard for him and Larissa to see each other." She opened the lipstick, made an O with her mouth, and smeared it more or less within the lines. "Her mother's boyfriend is a high-powered lawyer, which doesn't help. They're on a cruise in the Greek islands right now."

The lipstick was red—far too bright for my skin tone.

"I would never wear red lipstick!" I said. "Or that dress. You're making me look like a forty-year-old woman."

She blotted the lipstick with a tissue and blinked sadly. "I never got to be forty. I think I would have enjoyed it."

"Evelyn, this isn't about you!"

She raised her eyebrows. "I'm just trying to help you put your best face forward."

The final bell rang. We had to hurry. "What happened after Uno?"

"Claire—Larissa—that girl—she whined for a bit about her ex-boyfriend. He's way too old for her—nineteen or twenty, I wasn't really paying attention at that point—and he's moved on to someone else, but she still loves him, blah, blah, blah. Anyway, her mother is on a mission to keep her away from him. And from her father too. Maybe her father even more. Larissa wanted to stay with him this week, but her mother will do anything to keep them apart. That's why Larissa's here." She shrugged as if that were the end of the story, glossing over the little detail of how she, Evelyn, ended up in my body today.

"And?"

She squinted up at the clouds as if watching a bird fly away. "She fell asleep, finally. Her connection to your body started to loosen, until I could see her spirit drifting at the edges, like little puffs of smoke. The sooner she vacated the premises, the better, I figured, so when you didn't show up, I cuddled next to your body and slipped in. Larissa never felt a thing."

"And?"

She looked at me briefly and then at the ground. "I called Roger."

"Danish Roger?"

"He's not Danish, he's American. He just lives in Denmark. A lonely country, Denmark."

"How long did you and Roger talk?"

"An hour? Three? You might want to buy some more minutes for your cell phone."

"I didn't have enough minutes for a three-hour conversation to Denmark."

"True. You had enough for about twenty minutes. You shouldn't let your balance run so low. What would you do in an emergency? Anyway, Roger called me back on the home phone. We talked until the sun came up."

"You gave Roger our home phone number?" I took a deep breath and then another. I counted to ten and then I counted to twenty. And still I wanted to wring Evelyn's neck—except, of course, I'd be wringing my own neck, which would pretty much defeat the purpose.

"What time did you wake up?" she asked.

Prescott had come in shortly after sunrise. If she was being honest about when she went to sleep—a big if—then our sleep overlapped at least briefly.

"So we had at least twenty minutes," she said, as if that absolved her of any guilt. "Maybe even a half hour."

"Why didn't we switch, then?"

She shrugged. "I don't know. Maybe it took too much energy getting Larissa out of your body. Maybe a body can only take so many electrical changes at once. Or maybe it just wasn't long enough," she conceded. "I'll go to bed early tonight—pinky promise." She held up her pinky. "Everything will be fine. For now, let's just enjoy the moment."

She reached for her cigarettes. I held them behind my back.

I didn't feel as calm about the situation as she seemed to be. Evelyn had always said a switch was quick and painless, like a sneeze. She always insisted that the spirit is drawn back to its own body like iron filings to a magnet. Suddenly I knew there was something she wasn't telling me.

"What happened to you?" I asked her.

"When? Today?"

"No, years ago. When you went to . . . that place." Evelyn didn't like me to use the word *institution*. In fact, she didn't like to talk about "that episode," as she called it, at all, and always changed the subject when I brought it up.

"Or . . . weren't you the one there?" I asked.

Her mouth drooped. "It was me. Unfortunately."

"But what about before that? What happened to get you in there?"

She held up a hand and said what she'd always said: "You don't need to know about that."

"But maybe I do." This was no time to be polite or sensitive. I had to know the truth about switching. "You've always made it sound like it's easy to switch in and out of a body, that I'd never get stuck, but—"

"Larissa, is that you? I thought you were leaving today." I turned around and there was Nate, a blue backpack slung over his

136

shoulder. He looked at the package in my fist. "You smoke?"

"No! Of course not! They're . . . hers." I thrust the cigarettes at Evelyn. A smile twitched at her red lips. Then I remembered that Evelyn was *me*, and I wouldn't want Nate thinking I'd acquired such a vile habit. "I mean, we found them on the ground. We were just about to throw them away."

Evelyn took the pack and dropped it into her pocketbook, murmuring, "I'll stick them in the trash on my way out."

"Plans changed," I told Nate. "I'm here until tomorrow." Suddenly, that didn't sound so bad.

We stood there smiling at each other until Nate remembered his manners. He turned to my grandmother. "Hi, I'm—*Claire?*" Nate said, blinking. "I didn't recognize you at first."

Evelyn tilted her head to one side and smiled broadly. The red lipstick made my teeth look yellow. "I'm trying out a new look," she said. "What do you think?"

I cringed inside. I think I cringed outside too. I was actually embarrassed to be seen with myself. But Nate just grinned. "I think your makeup is going to get ruined in the pool. You're coming to practice, aren't you?"

"What practice?" I asked in Larissa's unpretty voice. "Trials aren't until tomorrow." Nate looked at me, confused. "I mean, that's what Claire told me, anyway," I added lamely.

Nate looked back and forth, uncertain which of us to address. "The coach called everyone last night. Said the pool would be open today."

"Oh, right. There was something on the machine," Evelyn said absently.

"You should go," I told her, even though she was better dressed for a funeral than swim practice.

"I don't really like the—" She stopped herself before she could say "water." She looked at Nate and then at me—and back at Nate. "I don't really like the first day of school. I think I'll just go home and lie down."

"Okay," Nate said, shrugging. "See you tomorrow."

As Evelyn walked away, I stared at him, stunned. Could Nate care so little about me that he wouldn't care whether or not I showed up for practice?

Suddenly, I pictured myself—not the way Evelyn had dressed me, in that freakish 1950s PTA style, but the way I usually look, in sweatpants or boys' jeans, with my big shoulders and boyish hips. It's not like I was hideous or anything, but how could I have imagined that someone like Nate Jameson could ever like me as more than a friend?

Someone came up behind me. "Hey, Nate, you going to practice?"

Beanie. She was eating a Snickers bar and carrying her Hawaiian-print beach bag, a striped towel sticking out of the top. Oh, Beanie. Sea-guard camp was one thing. Didn't she know that sports gear belongs in a duffel bag?

"I'll be there," Nate told Beanie. "You going?"

"Yeah, I figure I should at least check it out to see if I should bother with the trials tomorrow." She shifted the bag to her other shoulder and then turned her blue-eyed gaze to me. "Hi." She smiled.

If I didn't know her so well, I'd think she was being genuinely friendly, but I could see the hardness in her eyes, the hint of disapproval. You'd think girls could just get over the whole competition thing. It wasn't my fault that I was so perfect. I mean, that Larissa was.

"Hey," I said. It was so weird. On the one hand, I wanted to ask about her day: who was in her classes, if her teachers were okay. But on the other hand I felt like saying, "You have chocolate on your front teeth." And then I wanted her to go away.

"It's cool you're going out for swim team," Nate said to Beanie. "You've got a rockin' backstroke."

She blushed. "Oh, it's not that good."

Beanie was doing that thing she did—putting herself down so people would tell her that she was okay, she was worthy. If there's one thing that drives me crazy about her, this is it. I rolled my eyes. I didn't mean to—it just happened.

She saw it. The smile disappeared, and her face flushed deeper.

"Yeah, Beanie—it is *too* that good," Nate said.

I burned with shame. "Yeah, it's great," I added lamely, though of course Larissa had never seen her swim.

She took a step backward. "Okay. I'll see you at the pool, then." She gave Nate a final polite, Snickers-glazed smile. I couldn't let her walk around looking like that.

"Just to let you know?" I said.

Her smile disappeared.

"Your teeth." I made a little toothbrushing motion with my index finger. "They've got chocolate on them."

She narrowed her eyes and gave me a closed-mouth smile.

Actually, it was more like a sneer. She sucked on her teeth for a moment and mumbled, "'Bye, Nate," before walking away.

Around us, kids streamed past. More than a couple did a double take when they saw us. I tried to forget about Beanie, which should have been harder than it was.

"She's such a nice girl," Nate said. Then, "I could skip practice."

I shook my head. "No, it's important. You've got the trials tomorrow, not that you have anything to worry about, but still—you want to clock good times. We can meet up later, when you get out."

He ran a finger along my cheek. "It means so much to me that you would say that—that you would understand how important swimming is to me."

"I understand more than you can imagine."

I rode the bike home—to my real home, that is. Evelyn wasn't there. I'd seen her leaving school, packed into a decrepit car that spewed black smoke. *She'd better wear a seat belt*, I thought. *I don't want my body ending up in the emergency room.*

I let myself in the back and went up to check my computer: no messages. I was both relieved and hurt. Remembering Beanie's injured look, I felt a wave of guilt.

I typed a quick note:

Beans—Sorry to be such a freak today. Nice dress, huh? My mom really wanted me to wear it. Will explain tomorrow.

140

Fluffernutter was sprawled on the bed. I crept over slowly. His yellow eyes popped opened, but at least he didn't run away.

"Hey, Fluff." I stroked his white-and-orange fur until he rewarded me with a faint, rumbling purr.

My nose tickled, though not from sadness. Next, my eyes started to itch, and then they began to burn.

I stared at Fluffernutter with my swollen eyes. Larissa wasn't really allergic to bees—at least not as far as I knew—but her cat allergy was undeniable.

"Good thing I'm so hot-looking," I muttered. "Otherwise, this body would really piss me off."

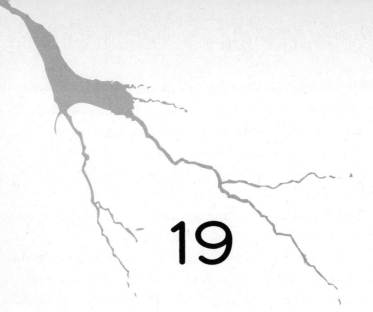

19

I SAW CAMERON FIRST, standing at the edge of the water in his orange swimsuit, shivering and hugging himself with his skinny pink arms.

"Come on in, Cam!" his father shouted. He was out in the waves with Prescott. When the water receded, the level came to Prescott's chin. *A kid who can't swim shouldn't be out that far*, I thought. His father held a rainbow-colored boogie board and looked out to sea, waiting for the perfect wave. Prescott faced the beach as a breaker snuck up behind him.

"Watch the wave!" I yelled—but it was too late. Prescott disappeared in a swirl of white, and then his head popped up, headed for the shore. He stood up, finally, the water now waist deep, and bent over, trying to cough the water from his lungs. A smaller swell rose from behind, knocking his feet out from under him. He washed up onto the beach.

"You okay, buddy?" Mr. Sealy called from the water. He had

tried to catch the wave but had failed and was still pretty far out.

Prescott nodded and coughed some more.

"That's my tough guy!" Mr. Sealy said.

Cameron, his face tight with fear, took a few steps backward onto drier sand.

Prescott got back on his feet, staggered up the beach, and grabbed a bright yellow donut-shaped floatie.

"That's just for pools," I said. "You shouldn't use it in the ocean."

Prescott stuck out his tongue. Good to see that he was back to his old self.

"Fine. Go drown," I muttered under my breath.

He stepped into the ring, holding it at his sides as he ran into the sea.

On the beach, Cameron was still hugging himself.

"Where's your mom?" I asked.

He shrugged his narrow shoulders.

I felt a sudden, unexpected stab of sympathy. "You want to make a sand castle?"

He turned to face me, his eyes suddenly wide with relief. He nodded and smiled, just a teeny bit.

Getting out of the house was easier than I expected. Mrs. Sealy was in her bedroom with the door closed: a migraine, Consuela told me, with a look that said one or all of the following: *Not that it's any of your business; Mrs. Sealy is a head case; I'd lock myself in a bedroom too if I had to live with this family.*

143

My clothes were sweaty from the bike ride, so I ran down to my room for a quick change—which turned out to be a not-so-quick change. Can you blame me? I mean, this girl had some seriously cute clothes! And they all looked great on me! (I mean, of course, on her.) The question wasn't, what looks good? But rather, *in what way* do I want to look good? The blue pinstripe miniskirt was totally adorable, but I didn't want to look over-dressed. The black halter top and denim miniskirt looked hot together, but the line between "steamy" and "trampy" was a little too thin for my comfort. Finally, I settled on a lacy peach camisole (innocent yet sexy), my favorite pair of Larissa's jeans, tight and faded (and unmistakably girl-cut), and the plaid Converse sneakers (an unexpected touch that screamed "spirited and fun-loving").

I didn't want to risk "borrowing" the bicycle again, so I walked to the high school. By the time I got there, Nate was the only one left in the pool. The air was thick and steamy and reeked of chlorine. I wanted to jump in a lane and start pounding the water so bad, my muscles actually twitched. Instead, I sat on a warm metal bleacher in the corner and watched Nate practice his freestyle. He looked like a dolphin. When he hit the end of the pool, he did a quick flip and shot back toward me, gliding underwater for a flash before shooting back to the surface. As he neared the end of the pool, the coach blew his whistle. Nate hauled himself up over the edge in one easy motion. He stood up and shook water out of his blond curls.

Guys on the swim team wear blue, knee-length lycra suits that can look hot or gross depending on who's wearing them. I'd seen

Nate in his suit countless times before, and there was no question that he fell into the "hot" category, but today my breath quickened. He was so beautiful, his tanned skin wet and shining under the buzzing fluorescent lights. His body had that triangle shape that male swimmers get, all shoulder and no hips. Unfortunately, female swimmers get that shape too. I pictured myself in my mother's black dress; thanks to Evelyn, I knew what *that* looked like. There is a reason I usually stick to jeans. I stretched out Larissa's long, long legs, loving them as if they were mine.

"Good turnout today," I heard the coach say to Nate. The coach was wearing what he always wears: a royal blue "Sandyland H. S. Athletics" polo shirt, khaki pants, and a whistle. Coach is a big guy, not fat, really, just—well, okay, he is kind of fat. But we all like him so much that no one would ever call him anything but "big." He's really dadlike—I mean, the way I always thought a father would be. He's got three daughters, one on the swim team and two in college.

"Should be a solid team this year," Nate said. He still hadn't seen me.

"What happened to Claire?" Coach asked. "I'm counting on her butterfly."

"I saw her after school," Nate said. My heart began to beat faster. I pictured Evelyn in her ridiculous outfit, a pack of cigarettes in her hand.

Coach scratched his head, his curly gray hair frizzing in the humidity. "I left a message for her last night. Never heard anything. I hope she's not flaking out on us."

Nate picked a towel off the floor and rubbed his hair. I leaned

145

forward, holding my breath. "She said she was feeling kind of sick. But she'll be here tomorrow."

I exhaled and closed my eyes with relief. Nate had covered for me. He really *was* my friend. When I opened my eyes, he was grinning at me from across the room.

I smiled back.

"Hey, dude," I said.

He crossed the tiles toward me. "Hey, babe." His voice echoed through the high-ceilinged room. "I didn't see you."

"I saw *you*," I said. "You looked awesome. In the water, I mean." I felt my face flush.

"You look awesome on land," he said, his smile growing even larger.

Coach looked from Nate to me and then back to Nate again. Then he laughed. "Don't stay out too late tonight, Jameson."

I waited outside while Nate showered and changed. The swim center was at one end of the school, set apart from the classrooms and the gymnasium.

The sun was low in the sky. It was getting chilly. I rubbed the goose bumps on my bare arms. In my old body, my real body, I didn't go anywhere without my red junior lifeguard sweatshirt, but today I'd been more concerned with looking good than with feeling good (but make no mistake: In the lacy peach camisole and skintight jeans, I looked *damn* good).

On the brick wall next to me, a glass-enclosed bulletin board advertised school clubs and activities. SIGN UP FOR SCHOOL CHORUS! SWIM TEAM TRYOUTS! STUDENT COUNCIL ELECTIONS COMING UP!

What did Larissa do in her spare time? I wondered. What was she missing out on by being in Sandyland rather than her hometown? (I tried not to think about what she was missing out on by not having a body.)

From what I could tell, she wasn't missing much. Maybe floating around in the ether was better than dealing with her crazy parents, her jerky ex-boyfriend, and her two-faced best friend. Maybe she didn't miss her life—or her body—at all.

Four boys approached, talking and laughing. I'd seen them around before—they were juniors, I think—but I didn't know their names. When they saw me, they slowed down. "Hey," one said, stopping to face me. He was about my height but much sturdier, his body almost square. He wore a black sweatshirt and baggy jeans that puddled at his feet.

"Hi." I smiled politely and looked at the ground.

"You new?" He took a step closer. His eyes were deep set in a puffy face, his hair brown and shaggy. Behind him, his friends snickered.

I shrugged: It was too complicated to explain.

"You a freshman?" he asked.

I clutched my arms more tightly and rubbed at my goose bumps. I'd give anything for my red sweatshirt. "I don't go here. I'm just visiting."

He stepped closer. "Maybe you can visit with me sometime." His friends burst into laughter. One of them whistled.

I felt a hand on my shoulder and jumped. It was Nate, wearing a navy blue "Sandyland Swimming" hoodie. His blond curls were still damp. "Sorry—didn't mean to scare you."

"You didn't. Just surprised me, is all." I turned away from the group of guys, knowing they wouldn't mess with me now. Nate smelled like shampoo mixed with chlorine. He put his arms around me, and we kissed for several seconds. I'd never kissed anyone but my mother in public before, and she didn't count. But then, until last night, I'd never kissed anyone at all.

Nate looked up; the guys were watching us. In a weird way, I was glad they were still there so I could show off, let them see what they were missing out on.

Nate nodded at them. "Hey." It wasn't a friendly greeting—more like a challenge.

The square-shaped guy put his hands in the pocket of his hoodie. "'Sup." He looked at the ground, and then he and his friends moved away.

I held Nate tightly and thought about how safe he made me feel—although until now I never needed anyone to make me feel safe.

"You feel cold," he murmured into my ear.

"I should have brought a sweatshirt."

"We can get one at my house. It's not far from here."

Nate's house was just a few blocks away—a tidy, mocha-colored Victorian surrounded by roses and hydrangeas. Over the summer, I'd ridden past it on my bike at least ten times, always hoping he'd be out front pulling weeds or something and I could say, "Hey, Nate! Do you live here?"

From there, I'd figured, we'd get to talking about swimming and high school and living in Sandyland, at which point it would be just a short leap to the moment when he'd realize he was madly in love with me.

As if.

He was never outside then, but now here I was as he fished a key out of his backpack and stuck it in the front door.

"Anyone home?" I hoped he'd say no. Nate lived with his mother. His parents were divorced, and his sister had just left for college. But since he hadn't told Larissa that, (officially) I didn't know.

"Doubt it," he said. "My mom usually manages to schedule a meeting around dinnertime." Nate's mother was running for a position on the school board, plus she volunteered with the recreation department, the Protect our Shoreline Foundation, and the Preserve Historic Downtown Sandyland committee. But again, I wasn't supposed to know this, even as Claire. Only a complete stalker would know that much about Nate's mother.

The living room was a disaster, with piles of papers on every surface, shoes on the floor, tote bags tucked in corners. There were brochures and posters for Mrs. Jameson's school board campaign, all with her slogan, "Putting Children First." Apparently, those children didn't include her own.

Nate dropped his backpack and sports duffel in the middle of the floor. "Be right back with the sweatshirt."

Bookshelves crammed with women's magazines, gardening books, swim trophies, and family photos flanked the fireplace. While Nate ran upstairs, I checked out the pictures. There was Nate smiling in his sophomore picture. I'd looked at this shot so many times in my yearbook, it automatically opened to that page. There was his sister in a graduation gown and hat. She was just normal-looking, not superhuman-gorgeous like her brother. There was Nate at the beach as a child (he bore a slight but nevertheless disturbing resemblance to Prescott) and Nate on a surfboard. I've never stolen anything in my life, but I had a sudden, overwhelming desire to sneak this photo out of the house.

Footsteps sounded overhead, and then Nate clomped down the squeaky stairs holding something red: the junior lifeguard sweatshirt. I gasped and then laughed.

"Is it okay?"

"It's perfect." I wanted to tell him that I had a sweatshirt just like it at home. Instead, I pulled it over Larissa's tiny camisole and immediately felt comfortable, not just in the shirt, but in Larissa's skin.

"Are you hungry?" he asked.

"Starving."

"How about some of my mother's famous home cooking, then?" He took my hand and led me into the kitchen, which was at least as messy as the living room, plus a little smelly. Time to take out the garbage?

He opened the freezer and pulled out a plastic-encased pizza. "Just like Mom used to make."

"My mom doesn't cook either."

"Sucks, doesn't it?" Nate wrinkled his nose—noticing the garbage smell, probably.

"Kind of. But now that I've learned to cook, we eat pretty well." I had a sudden urge to make him a meal.

"You cook?" His eyebrows shot up.

"It's not hard. I could make you something." *Oven-fried chicken*, I thought. *Macaroni and cheese.*

"Really?" He shoved the pizza box back into the freezer.

"Let's just see what you've got in here." Not much, it turned out, just some milk, Gatorade, prepackaged lunches, a sad-looking apple, a couple of cartons of Chinese food.

"You got any eggs?" I could make an omelet.

He peered inside. "Nope."

"Cheese?" Grilled-cheese sandwiches? Oh, yeah, we'd need bread.

"Nope . . ."

"Chicken, fish, meat?"

He straightened. "Does frozen Salisbury steak dinner count?"

"Well . . . no." I bit my lip. "You know what? Frozen pizza sounds awesome."

"Forget the frozen pizza. Let's get out of here."

By the time we got downtown, the sun was so low it cast a golden glow over everything. The walk had warmed me up, but I kept Nate's sweatshirt on. I never wanted to take it off. It was a size bigger than my own; the sleeves came all the way to my fingertips.

"Have you eaten anywhere downtown?" Nate asked me. There are only a few restaurants in town, none of them fancy. I'd eaten at every one of them, even the bad ones, more times than I could count.

"Nope," I said. "We mostly eat at the house."

We passed Romano's Pizza, which reeked of garlic; the Lobster Claw, which I've avoided ever since they served me a bad oyster a few years back; and Priscilla's Pancake House, which is only open for breakfast (duh); and then, the Burrito Bandito. My nose twitched. My mother brought home burritos at least once a week. I licked my lips. Larissa's tiny tummy needed a burrito, and it needed one now.

Nate stopped in front of the door. "This place is my favorite." (It was so hard not to say, "Mine too!") "But we could go somewhere else if you want."

"Oh, no—I love burritos!"

He beamed at me: I was beautiful *and* I loved burritos. What more could a guy want?

The Burrito Bandito is nothing great to look at: plastic yellow booths and a plain, white tile floor, but the food is killer. There was no one in line, so I walked right up to the counter. My tummy rumbling, I ordered my favorite thing without looking at the board. "I'll have a blackened chicken burrito, double rice, no beans, with roasted tomatillo salsa. Oh, and can you substitute fresh fruit for the salad?"

The guy behind the counter was pretty cute—not like Nate, but better than average—with wide brown eyes and thick dark lashes. He flashed me a super-white smile.

Nate gave me a weird look. I put a hand on his back to let him know that I was all his, that the counter guy meant nothing to me (though he'd do in a pinch).

"I thought you'd never been here before," Nate said.

Whoops. "I haven't. But . . . they have one of these in my

town. I know the menu by heart."

"Really? I thought this was the only one."

The counter guy said, "I don't think that—" But I shot him a wide-eyed, pleading (and super-pretty) look, and he stopped before blowing my cover. Instead, he flashed his bright, white smile and said, "I don't think the other Burrito Banditos are as good as this one."

"You may be right," I said, beaming back.

He ruined the moment by winking. Fortunately, Nate was looking at the menu. After he ordered his burrito (chili Colorado with chicken), I reached into my pocket for some money, but Nate said no. "I can't let you pay on our first real date."

Wow. Yesterday I had my first kiss, and now I was having my first date. I decided that it counted, no matter whose body I was in.

After he paid, we stepped to the side to wait for our food. A bell jingled as the front door opened. I almost screamed when my mother walked through the front door. She looked really harried, her long gray-and-brown hair slipping out of her braid. She wore khaki slacks, a pale blue blouse, and brown loafers. My mother needed a makeover even more than I did.

She blinked at me. "Larissa? Hi! How are you feeling?"

"Good," I said. "Fine."

My mother smiled at Nate. "You look familiar. From the summer program, maybe? I'm Claire Martin's mother."

"Right," Nate said, standing a little taller. "Hi, Dr. Martin."

I'd always wondered whether Nate was one of my mother's patients; now I knew that he wasn't. Just as well: The thought of my mother looking down Nate's throat, giving him his immunizations

153

and—oh, God—seeing him naked was just too weird.

My mother ordered a taco salad for herself. "And for my daughter, I'll also have a blackened chicken burrito with roasted tomatillo salsa, double rice, no beans, and fruit salad."

Nate squinted. "Isn't that what you . . . ?"

"Yeah," I said. "Weird. No wonder Claire and I get along so well."

"How'd you meet her, anyway?" he asked.

"Who, Claire? Just, you know. On the beach." I waited for him to say something, but he just nodded. "She seems really nice," I added.

"She is."

My mother paid for the food and went to sit at a yellow booth to wait. She caught my eye. I smiled and looked away.

I felt jittery all of a sudden, like I wanted to either sit down with my mother or flee onto the street. Being in the same room with her and pretending to be an almost-stranger was just too weird. What was Evelyn up to? I wondered for the first time in hours. She'd better be taking good care of my body.

"Is Claire's butterfly really as good as you said?" I asked Nate.

"Oh, yeah. Claire's the best. She swims better than most of the guys on the team."

I felt a sudden flash of pride in my old body—my real body—which was built for speed and strength.

"Plus, she's cool," he added.

(Me! Cool!)

"So, do you . . . like her?" My heart was pounding, my breathing shallow.

"Sure I like her." He shrugged. Then understanding passed over his face. "Oh, you mean do I *like* like her?" He laughed. "I like you. I thought that was kind of obvious."

"Well, yeah, it is." I looked down and scuffed the tile with my sneaker. "But if I weren't here, I mean, if you'd never met me, do you think you might like Claire?"

Nate bit his lip, searching for words. "Claire's a really nice girl. I just don't see her as, well—I guess I kind of see her as a guy." He laughed. When I didn't respond, didn't even smile, he tried to explain. "I mean, she's a girl, obviously, but she's the kind of girl you shoot baskets with, not the kind of girl you take out for a burrito." He reached over to touch my fair hair and I did my best to smile.

What did I expect—that he would confess peddling past my house, gazing at my yearbook picture, whispering about me with his best friend? Nate was a Golden Boy. Only a Golden Girl would do. It wasn't his fault; it was just the way things were. Right now I was lucky to be a Golden Girl, if only for a few days.

Still, it hurt. I looked around so I wouldn't have to meet his gaze. My mother was pushing buttons on her cell phone. She held the phone to her ear and bit her lip.

When our food came, Nate took the bag and walked to a booth. I followed him, my eyes flicking back and forth between my mother and Nate. She frowned at the cell phone and hit another button. She spoke for a bit and then closed the phone. Then she stood up and walked over to our table.

"Larissa? Nate? Have you seen Claire this evening?"

Nate shook his head. "Sorry."

155

"She isn't home?" Oh, crap.

"No. And she's not at her friend Beanie's house either. Swim practice wouldn't go this late, would it?"

"Uh-uh." Nate shook his head. "It ended over an hour ago. And Claire wasn't there anyway."

My mother's eyes widened. "She missed swim practice? That's not like her."

"She wasn't feeling well," I said. "Maybe she went home to lie down. Or out for some Tylenol or something." Or maybe she was drag racing or doing vodka shots or robbing convenience stores, or whatever those creepy kids did. I was going to kill Evelyn!

"Maybe," my mother said, though she obviously wasn't buying it. "If you see Claire, can you ask her to call me?" She hurried out the door with her food.

Nate left his burrito in its wrapper. "God. I hope Claire's okay."

"She's probably fine." I was doing my best to keep my voice steady.

"She seemed sort of . . . not herself today," he said.

Wow, he'd noticed me! He knew something was different! Maybe Evelyn's makeover wasn't so terrible after all.

"What did you think of Claire's dress?" I blurted.

"What dress?" So much for standing out in a crowd.

But right now, fashion was the least of my problems. I had to find Evelyn, and I had to find her now. "You know those kids Claire was hanging out with at school?"

"Huh? No."

156

"Those kids by the Dumpsters. I think one was named Jessamine?"

"Oh, I know who you mean."

I nodded. "Do you have any idea where they go after school?"

It would be tough to pick the prettiest place in Sandyland. There's the spot where the rock wall juts out into the ocean, standing tall against the battering white waves. There's the tiny harbor where the fishing boats moor, the water calm enough to reflect the sunset. There's the old downtown with its shingled buildings painted blue and yellow and peach.

Pinpointing the ugliest spot in Sandyland is easy.

"Why would they hang out at the mini-mart?" I asked Nate as we approached the asphalt parking lot.

He shrugged, one hand holding mine and the other clutching the bag of our unfinished burritos. "Because nobody else goes there?"

The mini-mart was built in the nineteen sixties, before the real-estate boom, back when Sandyland was just a sleepy town that happened to be on the ocean. The building was blah from the beginning, just a big, glass-fronted box in the middle of a treeless parking lot. It hasn't exactly improved with age. There's an auto repair shop on one side, a freeway ramp on the other.

We walked over to the side by the auto repair shop, and there they were, smoking by the Dumpsters. What was it with this crowd and Dumpsters? It was shadowy and kind of stinky: garbage mixed with cigarette smoke. The kids' voices bounced off the building's hard, gray wall. I squeezed Nate's hand, relieved to have him here with me.

"I don't see Claire," I whispered, panic growing

"Wait, isn't that her?"

It took a moment before I recognized myself. Evelyn had changed out of the black dress, thank God. Now she wore low-slung jeans and a tiny black shirt that exposed a strip of belly flesh. I'd always assumed I'd look stupid in clothes like that. As it turned out, I was right. (But then, tummy shirts look dumb on anyone. The jeans, I had to admit, showed off my butt nicely.)

The clothes were the least of it, however. As she crept out of the shadows, I stifled a gasp. I asked Nate to give us a minute alone and hurried toward her. A cigarette dangled from her fingers.

"Oops!" she said, dropping the cigarette on the pavement and grinding it out with her platform shoe. "Last one, I swear."

"What? Did you do? *With my hair?*" I said, once I'd dragged her away from the crowd.

It was red—orange, really. And not a nice shade of orange either—assuming there is a nice shade.

Evelyn patted her head. "It looks good, don't you think? You once said that you wished you'd gotten my hair, remember? Now you have!"

Her hair was loose, falling just below her shoulders. "You look like a different person," I said. I thought about waking up in my own body the next morning and having to go to school with that crazy hair. Beyond the swim lanes, I'd always tried to stay under the radar: Better to go unnoticed than to risk having people laugh at you.

But there was no time to make a stink. "Mom's on her way home. She's got dinner. You need to get out of here!" My mother. The hair. Oh, God.

She cocked her head to one side and tucked a gaudy strand behind her ear. "What's for dinner?"

"Burritos."

She scrunched her nose and shook her head. "I hate burritos."

"Have you ever even tried burritos?"

"I don't like foreign food."

"You love burritos," I said. "You especially love the kind of burrito she's brought home for you." I thought of Evelyn dying so young, of how my mother must have longed for her the way I longed for the father I'd never known.

"I'd think you'd be excited to spend an evening with your daughter," I said. "You said you didn't get to talk much this morning."

Evelyn pulled another cigarette out of her handbag and then, remembering her promise, dropped it back in. "I'm nervous," she said finally.

"Why?"

She bit her red lip. "I'm shy."

"You are *not* shy!"

"What if she doesn't like me?"

"Of course she likes you. You're me, remember?"

"I want her to love me for myself. All these years, I've been watching her, imagining the conversations we would have had, the things we would have done together. Shopping for shoes, getting our nails done, going out to lunch. Meeting her like

159

this—as you—it's just not the same."

I closed my eyes, too annoyed to respond. "She's going to ask about the hair," I said finally. "And the cigarettes. Make something up. Say it's a social studies experiment." It was a lame cover story, but it was all I could think of.

"I'm not going to smoke in front of her."

"It doesn't matter. You smell!"

Her brow wrinkled. "That was cruel."

I covered my face with my hands. "Aargh!" I took a few deep breaths and tried again. "Evelyn. You have to go home. Now."

"I don't feel ready to meet her." Her mouth quivered. "Besides, I've been stuck in that house for forty-two years. Do you really begrudge me a brief change of scenery?"

I gestured at the Dumpster. "Some scenery. Couldn't you find someplace a little nicer?"

She shrugged. "I was craving licorice. Besides, I had to buy another phone card, anyway."

"No more marathon phone sessions with Roger," I warned.

She smiled like an angel. "I'll be asleep by ten o'clock. I promise."

20

EVELYN WAS REALLY PISSING ME OFF, but there was no way she was going to ruin this evening for me. Tomorrow I'd be back to my old body and my boring life. Until then, I was going to make every second count.

"Maybe we should go with Claire," Nate said as we watched her wave good-bye to her Dumpster pals.

"She'll be fine." I waved my hand dismissively.

"We should probably make sure she gets home all right."

"What are you worried about? No one is going to hurt her." I swallowed. "Claire is big and strong. Remember? She's like a guy." And now, thanks to Evelyn, I looked like a guy in drag.

"I shouldn't have said that."

No, I thought. *You shouldn't have.*

"What I meant, I guess, is that hanging out with Claire is like hanging out with my guy friends. Easy, you know?" He took my hand and pulled me in the direction of Evelyn's—well, my—

161

retreating back. "How about if we follow behind? Just till she gets to her house."

I tried to turn off at the public beach, but Nate tugged me toward my street. Of course, I wanted to make sure Evelyn got home safely, but time with Nate was running out, and she'd already wasted too much of the evening.

I didn't think Evelyn knew we were following her, but when she reached the front door, she turned and blew us a kiss. "You kids have a swell time tonight!"

"Unbelievable," I muttered.

Nate waved back. When she'd disappeared inside the house, he asked, "Do you want to see my favorite place?"

I looked into his blue eyes and smiled. "I bet I know what it is."

"You think it's the beach."

I shook my head. "I went for a walk the other day and found this cove. There were fishing boats there. And a pier. Buoys and gulls. It was just really peaceful."

"Kimberley Cove—that's it!" Nate's eyes sparkled. "You're amazing."

(Disclosure: a couple of months earlier, I'd run into Nate on the pier, and he'd mentioned that the cove was his favorite spot in town. I went back every day for a week, but he never showed.)

"Sometimes I feel like . . ." He took a deep breath. "I feel like I've known you forever, like, maybe in a different life or something."

I squeezed his hand. "Funny. I feel that way too."

At the cove, we walked onto the pier, claimed a bench, and

finally opened the food bag. I tried not to think about Evelyn, who would be eating an identical burrito with my worried mother.

"Thanks for going with me to find Claire," I said.

"I didn't realize the two of you were so close," Nate said. "Didn't you just meet?"

"Yeah, but it feels like we've been friends for a long time." I watched a seagull battle a crab at the water's edge. "Claire and me—I guess you could say we're a lot alike."

"Yeah?" He squinted like he didn't see it. Then he smiled. "Maybe she's another friend from a former life."

The sky had turned a dusty pink. Small fishing boats entered the harbor, their wakes forming pink Vs behind them. The air smelled of salt and fish and gasoline.

We didn't talk much as we ate our lukewarm burritos, which felt right, somehow (the silence, not the burritos).

Finally, Nate crumpled up his wrapper. "My dad used to take me here when I was little. Back when he was still my dad."

"He's not your dad anymore?"

He shrugged. "He is, but I hardly ever see him. Spring break, New Year's, a week or two at the beginning of summer vacation. He moved to Chicago after he and my mom split three years ago. He's got another kid now—Christian. He just turned one. He's okay, I guess. But it's weird, when I see my dad, it feels like I'm borrowing him, like he really belongs to Christian."

I chewed my burrito slowly. *Which is worse,* I wondered: *to never have a father or to have one and then lose him?*

"I'm hardly ever allowed to see my dad," I said, thinking of

163

Larissa's letters from her father. I'd been thinking about Larissa's father a lot, which seemed strange since I'd never even met the guy. I told Nate what I knew: the missed alimony, the drinking problem, now under control. "He really wants to see me," I said.

"Does he know that your mother went on vacation and left you?" Nate asked.

"I don't think so."

He stood up and stretched. "Because I doubt that's allowed. The courts are pretty picky. If they hear that your mother took off, they might let you see your father." He held out his hand. I took it and stood up. We strolled back toward the shore.

"My mother is going to sell our house when I leave for college," he said. "It's part of their agreement."

I nodded, a lump forming in my throat. Nate would leave for college in two years. It seemed too soon. "Where do you want to go to school?"

He shrugged. "It doesn't matter where I want to go. All that matters is who gives me the most scholarship money." He put his arm around me, and our pace slowed. "I don't just swim for fun."

There was a clam shack at the beginning of the pier. We inhaled the aroma of greasy seafood.

"Maybe we should have skipped the burritos and had fried clams instead," he said.

"It's not too late," I said. "We could split a clam roll."

Nate squeezed my shoulders. "I'm so glad you have an appetite. I hate it when girls eat like rabbits."

I smiled. "I'm just lucky. I have a really fast metabolism."

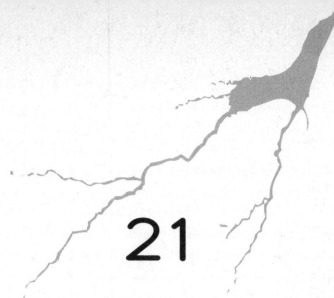

21

HERE'S WHAT I THOUGHT when I walked into the Ice Cube
House:

> *I will never love another boy the way I love Nate.*
> *I don't want to go back to my old life.*
> *I shouldn't have eaten the clam roll.*
> *I am in big, big trouble.*

I had come in from the road because it seemed less conspicu-
ous than climbing up from the beach. The front door was kept
locked at all times, but I knew the code: 1-2-3-4-5. Clever. What
thief would ever guess that one?

Before opening the door, I gave Nate a final wave good-bye.
He was standing by the curb, holding the red sweatshirt I had
given back. My lips still felt warm from our final kiss. I wouldn't
let him walk me to the door: too dangerous. I wouldn't give him

my cell phone or e-mail: even more dangerous. I had his e-mail on a slip of paper in my pocket.

I'd been hoping that the Sealys had gone out for dinner (I envisioned Mr. Sealy reading his newspaper in the middle of a restaurant), but the screaming and wailing hit me the moment I opened the door. They were all in the white, white living room with its soaring ceilings, Prescott sprawled on the concrete floor, pounding it with his fists, Cameron clutching his mother's waist and sobbing. Mrs. Sealy stood stock-still, hands over her face, tears leaking out the edges, while Mr. Sealy sat at the stainless-steel table, typing on a laptop and acting as if nothing was wrong.

"Where were you?" Mrs. Sealy shrieked when she saw me.

"Out?" I said.

"I needed you! The boys are overtired and cranky, and they've been just awful! It's one tantrum after another." Her voice cracked. "I can't do this on my own, I just can't!"

"Sorry?" I said, as if that would take care of everything.

Mr. Sealy continued to type. Prescott continued to scream. Mrs. Sealy grabbed Cameron's hands and pried them away from her waist. "Larissa's going to put you to bed," she told him without looking at me. "She's going to put you to bed *now*."

"I don't wanna go to bed!" Prescott howled.

"I need to lie down," Mrs. Sealy said, stumbling toward the stairs. "My head! Oh, my God—my head."

"MOMMY!" Cameron shrieked, running after her.

"Mommy needs to lie down!" She ran up the shaky stairs. Above us, the door slammed.

Cameron crumpled to the floor. He sat there, slouched and

crying, though not as loudly as before. Prescott let out an animal wail, but his volume was dying down, as if he'd run out of energy.

"Well," Mr. Sealy said, finally looking up. He closed his laptop and pushed back his chair. "I think I'll go out."

"Okay," I said. I expected Prescott to protest, but he had grown almost lifeless.

Mr. Sealy stood and plucked his keys off the shiny counter. "See you later."

The boys and I stared at the door for a moment after Mr. Sealy closed it behind him. Then they turned to me with wary expressions.

"Who wants to hear a mermaid story?" I asked, feeling desperate. I didn't know any mermaid stories. Actually, I didn't know any stories at all. When I babysat around town, I usually read Dr. Seuss or something, but if there was a single book in the Ice Cube House, I hadn't seen it. To make things worse, my stomach felt more awful by the minute. It was bad enough that Larissa was allergic to cats. I had a horrible suspicion that she was allergic to clams too.

The boys hadn't answered my question, but at least they were quiet. Clearly, they wanted to hear the story, but they didn't want to give in too easily.

"Okay," Cameron said, finally.

"You can only hear a mermaid story if you're in your pajamas and your teeth are brushed." Prescott opened his mouth to protest, but I cut him off. "It's the rule of the sea."

Prescott squinted at me, not convinced that a story was worth brushing his teeth. Were mermaids not exciting enough? Did he need a little violence? "There are pirates in the story," I said. "Okay?"

He took a deep breath and then let it out loudly. "Okay."

This was my story:

"Once upon a time, there was a girl who loved the ocean so much that she wished she could swim underwater with the fish and the dolphins and never come up for air."

"Dolphins come up for air," Cameron interrupted. "I've seen them."

I'd tucked the boys into their matching twin beds and was sitting on the floor between them.

"I never said they didn't. I just said the girl didn't want to have to come up for air. So, anyway, one night the girl went to sleep, and when she woke up she was at the bottom of the ocean—and she could breathe! She saw beautiful fish—orange fish and blue fish and silver fish. When she looked down, she saw that she had grown a big fish tail where her legs used to be. A dolphin swam by. She grabbed his fin, and he took her for a ride."

"Were there sharks?" Cameron asked.

"No sharks."

"There would be sharks," Prescott said. I ignored him.

"So, anyway," I continued, "the girl lived underwater for two days and had the most wonderful time, but then she started to miss life on land. She missed the sunset and she missed her school, but most of all she missed her mother. So she went to sleep, and when she woke up she was just a girl again. The end."

Not bad, I thought. *Not bad at all.* I stood up and gave each boy a kiss on the forehead.

"You forgot the pirates," Prescott said.

"Pirates. Right." Would I never get out of here? "When the girl was underwater, she found a huge treasure chest that pirates had left behind. She kept some of the gold. After that, she and her mother were really rich so they took a vacation in Hawaii. The end."

The pains in my stomach were growing sharper. I felt like I was going to throw up.

"No fair," Prescott said. "Treaure's not the same as pirates."

"Okay," I said. "Fine." I took a deep breath and put a protective hand on my belly. "When the pirates discovered that the girl had stolen the treasure, they set sail for Hawaii, where they found her taking surf lessons. They grabbed her and took her on board the ship and made her walk the plank, and she drowned. The end."

"But she's a mermaid!" Cameron gasped. "Mermaids can't drowned!"

"Drown," I said. "No 'd' on the end unless you're using the past tense. She wasn't a mermaid anymore, remember? She was just a girl. So she drowned." I shrugged. Cameron started to cry.

"I was just kidding!" I said. "Geez! Okay, you're right. She turned into a mermaid again and her dolphin friend came and gave her a ride back to her home, and she and her mother lived happily ever after."

"I like it better when she dies," Prescott mumbled.

✕

Once I'd turned out their light, I changed into the oversize gray T-shirt (Consuela had washed it) and a pair of sweatpants. It felt like I should be packing, like I should bring a suitcase along for the upcoming voyage back to my body. At least my own stomach wouldn't hurt (though I was worried about my lungs after all the smoking Evelyn had done). There was soda in the refrigerator upstairs; maybe a ginger ale would help settle the clams.

I crept up the stairs to the main level. The great room was just the way we'd left it, only without the sounds of screaming, whining, and moaning. The room was cool and breezy and smelled of the sea. The crashing waves were louder than usual, as if a storm might be moving in. Wonderful. That's all I needed: to switch out of Larissa's body only to get knocked into someone else's. Then again, maybe I'd wind up here again. Hmm . . .

I got a ginger ale out of the buzzing stainless steel refrigerator and popped it open. It helped a little. Mr. Sealy's laptop was still sitting on the table. I tiptoed over and touched the computer carefully, as if it might shock me. It didn't. I went to the front door and peered through the peephole: no sign of Mr. Sealy.

My heart pounding, I hurried over to the laptop, opened it up, and hit the power button. It didn't ask for a password; it logged me right on. I shook my head in disgust; people are so naïve when it comes to electronic security.

Within minutes I had a new e-mail address and Internet identity: Rapunzel. I hit COMPOSE and entered the e-mail address Larissa's father had given her.

Dad,
I think there is something u should know. I am not
@ home now. I am in a little town called Sandyland
staying w/ the Sealys. I am here 2 babysit their 2
boys but mostly I think I am here so Mom can go on
a cruise. Can she do that? Just leave me with other
people w/o telling u?
I miss u & I love u.
Larissa.

I hit SEND and ran back to the peephole: still no sign of Mr.
Sealy. I couldn't imagine where he had gone. There was nothing open at this time of night except the mini-mart. The
thought of him hanging out by the Dumpsters made me smile.
Next I crept to the stairs that led up to the master bedroom: no
sounds from Mrs. Sealy. Ditto for the boys and Consuela, who,
as far as I could tell, shut her door at eight o'clock every night
and didn't open it again until morning. She must have a really
big bladder.

At the computer, I logged on to my own e-mail account.
Whether I liked it or not, tomorrow I'd be Claire again. Might as
well start cleaning up the mess Evelyn had made.

Beanie.
u must think I'm a crazy person. u may be right,
LOL. I didn't want 2 tell u, but this is all part of an
experiment I am doing 4 school. I think I want 2 b a
psychologist when I grow up so I thought it would

be fun 2 c how people would react. w8 till u c my hair!
Sorry if I hurt ur feelings. I should have told u
sooner. u r still my best friend & always will b.
xo, Claire

I sent the message, knowing that it sounded weak but hoping Beanie wouldn't question it, and did the peephole/upstairs/downstairs routine again before logging back on as Rapunzel.

Nate,
Please don't come by the house. It will only cause
trouble. Remember me every time you go to
Kimberley Cove. I am closer than you think.

I was about to sign the message from Larissa, but I was already starting to feel jealous of her. Instead, I simply signed it, "Rapunzel."

That's it, I thought: *no more fabulous clothes, no more admiring stares, no more Nate.* If only we'd made plans to meet up later—I could have snuck out. If only I could feel beautiful for a little while longer.

There was no point in stalling. I had to go home.

Five minutes later, the ginger ale finished, the computer shut off, I was back in Larissa's room. I took one last, loving look in the closet mirror before settling into bed and falling into a deep, deep sleep.

22

I KNEW IT BEFORE I EVEN OPENED MY EYES. The smell was wrong: new paint instead of faint mildew. The sounds were wrong: muffled waves instead of noisy finches. My stomach was wrong: it still felt slightly queasy, though not as bad as last night.

I was still Larissa.

"Nate," I whispered to the empty room.

The boys were letting me sleep in, for once. It was six thirty and they hadn't come in to catch a glimpse of me in my underwear. Of course, I was wearing the gray T-shirt, so maybe they'd already peeked and left disappointed.

I dashed to the closet and checked the mirror. My blond hair was wild from sleep, my cheeks were flushed. I laughed. It was just wrong that anyone could look this good first thing in the morning. *Another day*, I thought. *I get another day.*

Imagine you've had this fab vacation—in Hawaii, say, at a hotel with koi ponds and waterfalls—and your suitcase is packed and you're all sad about going back to your boring house and your boring school. But then, on the day you're supposed to leave, your mother says, "Surprise! School can wait—we're staying an extra day!" And then you put on your shades and bikini, and you're just exploding with joy because you know that this is going to be the Best! Day! Ever!

That's just how I felt, except for one itty-bitty problem. I wasn't in Hawaii, and I wouldn't be missing school, at least not technically. How much trouble would Evelyn get into today?

I pulled on a hoodie sweatshirt, the plaid sneakers, and a pair of gym shorts that said "Juicy" on the butt. Larissa's cell phone was in the drawer; I stuck it in the hoodie pocket, just in case.

After leaving a note that would probably get me in trouble ("Taking a run"), I jogged through the foggy streets until, sweaty and winded, I reached my house. The sun was just starting to break through. The newspaper was gone from the front walk, which meant my mother was up. But the blinds on my bedroom window were shut even though Evelyn should have been getting ready for school. Swim team trials were today, I remembered with a pang.

I crept around to the back and peeked in a window. My mother, wearing her faded blue flannel bathrobe, was making coffee. Most days she'd be dressed by now.

I tiptoed to the side of the house and pulled out the cell phone.

"Hello?" my mother answered, sounding concerned.

"Hi, uh—Mrs. Martin?" Pretty smooth, pretending not to know she was a doctor.

"Yes?"

"My name is . . ." I looked at the plant next to me. "Rose." Above me, a bird began his morning song. "Rose Finch. I live on the street behind you? Hate to bother you, but I'm expecting a package, and the shipping company thinks they delivered it to your house by mistake. It would be in your garage. Could you check?"

"Of course," my mother said, as I'd known she would. The word *no* is not in my mother's vocabulary. "If you'll just hang on a minute, I'll—"

"I have to run, but if you'll just leave the package out front, I'll pick it up later. Thanks!" I hung up.

On cue, the back door opened, and my mother, wearing green rain boots with her bathrobe, clomped across the yard to the garage. I ran for the front door, which my mother always left unlocked after bringing in the morning paper.

Evelyn was still asleep, the air around the bed eerily cold. Was Larissa hovering? I wondered. I wished I had worn something nicer than the hoodie. I wouldn't want her to think I was slacking off in the fashion department.

"Wake up!" I whispered, shaking Evelyn.

"Whaa . . . ?" She blinked and pushed her newly red hair from her face. My face. "Claire?"

I nodded.

She held up her hands, inspected the nails. (How long had they been red?) She let her arms fall back on the bed and moaned. "Shoot. I was afraid of this."

I opened the blinds, and fog-tinged sunlight flooded the room. "Why are you still here?"

"You're not going to school today," she said, still lying down. "I was going to tell you—assuming you were yourself this morning. And your mother's not going to work. She scheduled an emergency appointment for this morning. With a shrink. I hate shrinks." She rolled over and closed her eyes. "It didn't go well between the two of us last night. She made a big deal about the cigarettes, and about me missing swim practice and staying out with my friends." Her voice cracked. "I don't think she likes me."

I sat on the edge of the bed and leaned over her. "What I meant is, why are you still *in my body?*"

She rolled back and shifted until she was kind of sitting up. "I don't know. It doesn't make any sense. Unless . . ."

"What?"

"Unless it's because you really want to stay in that body. Emotions, if they're strong enough, can create a kind of energy all their own. Envy, desire . . ." She held my eyes. "Love."

I was beginning to wonder if Evelyn really knew what she was talking about or if she was just making it up as she went along. Besides, I'd had some good times as Larissa, but it wasn't as if I wanted to be her forever. Was it?

"Then there's the deal with your birthdays," Evelyn said, pushing herself up farther. "You two weren't just born under the same moon. You were born under the same sun."

"I was born at night."

"So was she. I asked her. About an hour after you. That's got to make the connection stronger. Still." She tucked a strand of orange hair behind her ear. "I thought you'd be back by now—I

176

hoped you would. I got you invited to a party this weekend, and I don't want you to miss it. Besides, I'm not crazy about the whole psychiatrist thing. My last experiences with the mental-health profession . . ." She left the sentence unfinished, but I could suddenly see the white coats, the restraints.

"It wasn't you," I said, "was it? The one who went crazy, I mean. The one who got committed and went to the hospital." I began to shake. "You got stuck in someone else's body, didn't you? *Didn't you?*"

She stared at the ceiling for a long time before she finally spoke. "It was really me in the hospital. But you're right. I wasn't the one who went crazy."

"So I may be stuck this way?" My voice cracked and my eyes teared up, whether from panic or Larissa's cat allergy, I didn't know. A few more days as Larissa would be okay—actually, it would be fun—but forever?

"This is different." Evelyn shook her head. "Larissa doesn't want your body. And neither do I. No offense."

"What happened to you?" I asked, ignoring the insult.

"I don't like to revisit that time."

"You have to tell me!"

My mother's footsteps sounded on the stairs. Evelyn and I stared at each other, and then I made a dash for the closet.

"You awake?" I heard my mother say through the closed closet door.

"Mm," Evelyn grunted from the bed.

"You should get up soon."

"Mm."

177

"I'm going to take a shower. Will you be okay until I get out?"

"Mm-hm."

A moment later, I was back by the bed. "You owe me the truth."

23

HERE'S WHAT EVELYN TOLD ME:

Barb Root was born forty-two minutes before her, but they didn't know that until their twenty-sixth birthday, when my grandfather took Evelyn, hugely pregnant with my mother, out for a candlelit dinner. They had just finished their food: baked halibut and mashed potatoes for my grandfather, fried cod and steak fries for Evelyn, coleslaw with both. These were pre-Burrito Bandito days, when nothing said "special occasion" like a big mound of slaw.

After dinner, my grandfather nodded to the waitress. Within minutes she was at the table holding a mongo chocolate cake and singing "Happy Birthday." Evelyn considered her wish. Since she already had everything she ever wanted, she hoped for a healthy baby and an easy delivery.

She took a deep breath, craned her neck over her enormous belly, and—

"Today's my birthday too!" came a voice from across the room.

Evelyn sputtered, blowing out fewer than half the candles. She was totally freaked out by the interruption. What if she'd blown her chances for a healthy baby and an easy delivery? (The baby was healthy, of course, and the delivery probably wasn't as bad as she said it was.)

Then she looked up at the intruder, a bony young woman with thin lips and a beaklike nose. "She looked like a mean bird," Evelyn told me. "The kind that swoops down and carries off bunnies."

But my grandfather was all, "What a pleasant surprise!" And, "Happy Birthday, Barb!" And, "You must join us!" My grandfather had known Barb Root since they were young, even though she'd been four years behind him in school. Back then, Sandyland was even dinkier than it is now.

Evelyn had grown up in a small city a couple of hours away, far from the ocean. She'd met my grandfather as he was finishing up his medical training at the local hospital. When they'd married, the year before, she'd been happy to move to a small town because there would be fewer women born under the same moon. She hadn't counted on there being so many more thunderstorms closer to the ocean.

And she hadn't counted on Barb Root.

Within minutes the three of them determined that Barb and Evelyn were born less than an hour apart. Barb thought this was nifty. Evelyn, not so much. On the plus side, Barb lived with her mother almost four miles away, up in the hills—too far to switch.

180

Barb accepted a slice of cake but let it sit there while she sucked on one cigarette and then another, ogling my grandfather through the smoke.

"You have no idea how lucky you are," she told Evelyn. "You have no idea how many girls in Sandyland would give their eye-teeth to be Missus Doctor Martin."

After they left the restaurant, Evelyn was oddly silent. "Penny for your thoughts?" my grandfather said. (You'd think he'd be grateful that she'd stopped talking for once.)

"That . . . woman."

"Oh, Barb means no harm." My grandfather laughed. He took Evelyn's hand. "You have nothing to worry about. I promise."

But the promise wasn't his to make.

"It happened a few years later," Evelyn told me. "On the Fourth of July. Your mother was three. We looked so cute that day, in our matching red-and-white-striped shirts and our starred headbands. Once it got dark, the three of us went to the beach to watch the fireworks, which weren't wonderful—it was too cloudy. I was afraid the noise would make your mother cry, but she was a tough little cookie—just covered her ears and said, 'Ooh, pretty flower!' every time a firework bloomed in the sky."

"Barb was there," I said.

She nodded. "Early on, she came over to say hello. She was one of your grandfather's patients now, and she made this big deal, thanking him for being so understanding about her headaches, her back pain, and her unexplained dizzy spells." Evelyn wrinkled her nose. "Barb's health really went in the toilet once she changed doctors."

Evelyn's eyes—my eyes—turned glassy with tears. In this light, they looked more green than hazel. Pretty, even.

"The storm came up suddenly," she said. "Or maybe it wasn't so sudden. It was hard to see behind all the smoke from the fireworks." She took a deep breath. "And that was it."

"What was it?"

"I got stuck." She blinked away the tears. "We switched, Barb and I, right there on the beach. Her friend drove me home—Barb lived with her mother—and I went to sleep in her room. So tacky, with magazine pictures on the wall and afghans draped over everything. I tried not to get too upset, figuring I'd wake up as myself, but . . . no. Day after day, I was Barb, complete with her nicotine addiction, pinch-faced mother, and mind-numbing job as a supermarket checker. And she was me.

"I went to see her at my house, of course, assuming she'd be as upset as I was, as anxious to get back to her life, but . . ."

"She wasn't."

"Quite the contrary. She had this twisted idea that the switch was meant to be, that she deserved my husband, somehow, because she'd had a crush on him for so long. I think it was her desire that kept her in my body, the very force of it.

"I started putting pressure on her, showing up at the door and even sleeping in the yard a couple of times, thinking maybe if I was closer to my body . . . It just about killed me, watching this woman steal my life—chain-smoking in front of the television, just completely neglecting my daughter. She yelled at me, threatened to call the police. But she didn't, of course. She was too afraid they'd discover she was a fraud, that she'd lose the life she had stolen. Finally, she cracked—just went off the deep end, so agitated that all she could do was scream and cry. I heard that she locked herself in the bedroom and refused to come out.

"Your grandfather was overwhelmed. Plus, he was afraid she'd hurt your mother." She covered her mouth. "He felt he had no choice," she said through her fingers.

"He had her committed," I said.

"Yes. The funny thing is, I was glad! I wanted that woman out of my house, away from my husband and daughter, whatever the cost."

"Was she there when you died, then?" I asked. "In your body, I mean?"

She shook her head. "Once she was institutionalized, she didn't want my body anymore. Plus, the hospital wasn't far from Barb's house. The very first night, she released her hold. I was me again."

"Terrific," I said wryly.

"Yeah. Whoopee. I thought, 'I'll be out of here in no time!' But I couldn't convince them that I was A-okay and ready to go home. Barb had changed me too. After all her chain smoking, I was a nicotine addict, just like her. Cigarettes were the only thing that controlled my jitters. Plus, the longer they kept me in there, the more upset and angry I got."

She fingered the bedspread. "Electroshock therapy was a popular treatment back then. Maybe it worked for some people. But for a switcher . . ."

"My God," I whispered. I'd seen what a little spark of static electricity could do.

"It sent me right out of myself," she said softly. "At first I floated over the hospital, but after a few days of living without a soul, my body simply . . . died. My spirit thinned out and blew back to my old house." Her gaze swung around the room. "And here I am. Still."

I reached out and took her hand. It was a strange sensation, like when one of your arms falls asleep, and you stroke it with your other fingers. It's like touching you and not-you, at the same time.

"There's one more thing you should know," Evelyn said, squeezing my hand.

I wasn't sure I could handle one more thing.

"I met a couple of people at the hospital. Patients. And maybe they were truly crazy, or maybe it was because of all the drugs they gave us. But what they were talking about, the things that happened to get them committed . . ." She paused to look me in the eye. "It sure as heck sounded like switching."

It took me a moment to process this. "So it's not that unusual?"

"In the general population, yes—extremely. But in mental hospitals, maybe less so. One of the patients had only switched once or twice, but talking about it still got her locked up. Understand, Claire: You must never tell anyone about your switching. Never."

I nodded, unable to speak.

"I probably should have told you all of this sooner," she said, smoothing the bedspread over her legs. "But I didn't want you to be scared."

"Too late for that now." My voice shook. Around us, dust particles danced in the air, glinting from the sunlight. "Though this is probably even scarier for Larissa."

I glimpsed her pale face, looking back from the mirror. "Wherever she is."

24

CONSUELA WAS JUST STARTING BREAKFAST when I got back to the Ice Cube House. She barely said hello, apparently forgetting that yesterday we had been on the verge of friendship. Mr. Sealy was out on the deck, reading the paper and ignoring his sons, who were crawling around at his feet. Beyond him, the waves crashed violently.

"Is Mrs. Sealy still sleeping?" For one brief moment, I believed in luck.

"Yoga," Consuela said.

"Ah." I slipped my jogging note off of the counter.

Consuela nodded at the note. "She see that. She mad."

Downstairs, I lay on the white comforter and stared at the ceiling. I didn't even realize I was crying until I felt a tear slide down the side of my face. Another followed and then another, until my pillow was soggy. What was wrong with me? The night before, I dreaded being Claire again, couldn't stand the thought of losing the hair, the legs, the clothes—and, of course, Nate. But suddenly I missed my mother as if I hadn't seen her in years, and I felt bad about how upset she must be. I wanted to call Beanie to say that I'd seen Avon and Ryan sucking face on the beach. I wanted to fly through the water in the time trials, with Nate there to see me, even if he'd never look at me the same way again.

Evelyn's story had scared me, all right. How was I going to get out of here? What was I supposed to do? Stick a fork in a socket? Play golf in a thunderstorm?

Finally, I got up, washed my face, and changed into the brown bikini. I left my running clothes on the floor in case Mrs. Sealy should peek in. I pulled a different pair of shorts over the bikini and was astonished to find them a little tight at the waist—payback for all of those burgers and burritos.

Upstairs, Consuela was loading a tray with fruit, pancakes, eggs, and orange juice. The square white plates—three of them—were stacked on the counter, the tray too full for them to fit. I picked up the plates. "I'll take these out."

Consuela raised an eyebrow, shrugged. "Okay."

I followed Consuela out to the deck. Immediately, the wind blew the paper napkins off of her tray.

"I'll get more," I murmured, placing the plates on the table and going inside to retrieve more napkins.

When I came back out, Cameron had taken a seat as far from his father as possible. I handed him a napkin, which he placed on the table only to watch it blow away. I held my finger up in a "shh" sign: No one had noticed.

Mr. Sealy folded his newspaper and squinted at me. I handed him a napkin. "Thanks," he said, surprising me with something resembling manners.

It was too quiet. "Hey, Cameron, where's Prescott?"

Cameron twisted his head to peer around the deck. He shrugged.

"Mr. Sealy?" I said carefully. "Have you seen Prescott?"

A forkful of egg had almost reached his mouth. He put the fork back on his plate. "He was just here."

I ran to the edge of the deck and looked at the grass below. There was no sign of him. "Prescott?" My heart began to beat faster.

Mr. Sealy dropped his paper on the table and joined me at the side of the deck. "Prescott? Answer me!"

I dashed down the deck stairs, not bothering to check under the deck or around the house, not wasting an instant looking in the bathroom or under the beds. If he were in any of those spots, an extra minute or two wouldn't matter.

I saw him as soon as I reached the rock wall—or, rather, I saw his bright yellow floatie, and then, to my relief, I saw his little blond head in the middle of it. He was beyond the breakers, drifting out to sea.

"Prescott!" The wind blew my voice back in my face. My long blond hair tangled and swirled, the strands stinging my face.

"He's in the water!" I yelled to Mr. Sealy, who had just reached the bottom of the deck stairs. We sprinted down the concrete steps to the beach.

"Stay here—I'll get him!" he yelled. Still wearing his polo shirt and khaki shorts, he plunged into the surf.

I stood poised at the edge of the water, blood rushing through my ears. Down here, with the waves blocking my sight line, it was harder to see Prescott. A breaker hit Mr. Sealy. He went under for a moment and then reemerged, fighting the water with a sloppy crawl stroke.

The floatie was growing smaller now. Mr. Sealy was nowhere close. Even worse, he was angling in the wrong direction.

Cameron sat at the top of the stairs, clutching his knees to his chest. "Is Prescott gonna drowned?" he whimpered.

"No!" How could anyone drown with me around? For five years in sea-guard camp, I'd been preparing for this moment.

The boogie board lay on the grass. I grabbed it and bounded back down, attaching the Velcro strap to my wrist.

The water, always cold, seemed extra-frigid today. The currents must have shifted with the incoming storm. Even if Prescott managed to cling to the floatie, he would only last for so long.

I dove under one breaking wave and then another, the boogie board strap yanking at my arm. Past the breakers, I saw a flash of yellow. I wasn't going as fast as I wanted, my arms were aching, and I was almost out of breath.

Mr. Sealy was in even worse shape, gasping for air and slapping at the water. I suddenly realized he was fighting a riptide, trying to outmuscle the sea. It was pulling me out too, the Ice Cube House shrinking in the distance.

When I caught up to Mr. Sealy, I ripped the Velcro from my wrist. "Take the board."

"No!" He gasped. "Forget about me. Just get Prescott!"

I shoved the board in his direction. "Shut up and take it! And stop fighting the current!"

My chest hurt from the strain of breathing. My arms and legs would have ached from exhaustion if they weren't so numb from the cold. I flipped on my back and kicked, letting the current propel me toward Prescott. Finally, I was within a few strokes of the floatie. It popped up on a wave: empty. A gust lifted the yellow ring and blew it beyond my reach.

"Prescott!" Treading water, I yelled into the wind, a sob catching in my throat.

To my astonishment, I heard a cry in return. I rode up on a swell. On the other side, Prescott was just managing to hold his head above water. I kicked over, only to see him disappear under a wave. I dove down, grabbing Prescott's tiny body. I pulled him up and flipped him on his back.

"Just let me hold you, Prescott! And keep floating!" A wave splashed his face. He sputtered but didn't cry, didn't speak.

I tried to swim parallel to the beach, to get him out of the riptide and tow him to shore, just like I'd practiced a million times with fake drowners far larger than this little boy. But I couldn't do it. Larissa's body—the beautiful body with the flat tummy, slim arms and endless legs—was done. My knowledge and willpower could only do so much. I was exhausted.

A wave reared up and knocked us under the surface. We came up gagging on salt water. I expected Prescott, that tough and noisy kid, to cry or yell, but he only coughed weakly. My breathing was out of control. Prescott's lips were blue at the edges.

What would happen if I died in Larissa's body? Would I float around in the ether like Evelyn, a soul without a body to call home? Or would I condemn Larissa to that fate?

If this were a fairy tale and I were a princess, a prince on a shining white horse would have come riding out to rescue me. Horses can swim, after all. Instead, my prince appeared on a surfboard. The World's Safest Beach finally had some swells, and Nate had hoped to catch a few waves before heading to class.

My relief was so great that it wasn't until later that I remembered how much I despised princess stories.

"His dad," I gasped.

"Onshore already," Nate said.

Nate pulled Prescott onto the surfboard; I clutched the back. He paddled parallel to the land until we were out of the current, then we rode a wave to the beach.

Nate dragged Prescott out of the water and laid him on the sand. He bent his head to Prescott's face, seawater streaming from his blond curls, and listened for breathing. Then he began artificial respiration: one, two, three breaths, and pause; one, two, three, and pause.

My heart pounded, my lungs ached. I wanted to be the one breathing for Prescott, but there was nothing I could do but sit there, helpless and shivering.

A man with a dog appeared, and then an older couple. "Call nine-one-one," I wheezed.

"We already did." They handed me their jackets, which I wrapped around Prescott. "Put one on yourself," the woman said.

I shook my head. "I'm okay." My body trembled. I was cold, so cold. "Call my mother." I gasped, water dripping from my masses of hair.

"Who's your mother?"

"Dr. Martin. Call her." And then I watched as Nate breathed life back into Prescott.

25

HERE ARE SOME OF THE THINGS I SAID LATER, at the health clinic, where my mother—Claire's mother—insisted I spend a few hours for observation:

"I don't know how I learned to swim. Nate gave me a lesson. Maybe that was it."

"When I said 'call my mother,' what I meant was, call Claire's mother. My mother isn't here. My mother is on a cruise."

"I'm just glad that Prescott is okay. That's all that really matters."

My mother said Prescott would have died if he'd spent another minute in the water. The ambulance crew said Prescott would have died if my mother hadn't gotten there five minutes before them. What nobody said was that Prescott would have died if I hadn't switched with Larissa. But it's true, isn't it? The real Larissa wouldn't have noticed Prescott missing. She would have been busy painting her toenails or working on her tan.

Then again, who knows? Maybe she would have been down

on the beach with the boys, and the whole thing never would have happened.

Nate said I was a hero: If I hadn't held Prescott up for those last few minutes, he would have drowned. And that's true, I guess. But if Nate hadn't shown up, Prescott and Larissa would both be dead, and her beauty would have been of no use to anyone.

Nate stayed with me at the clinic, his arm around me the whole time. I had changed into scrubs, the only dry clothes available. A blue blanket and Nate's arm kept me warm. While walking across the beach with his surfboard that morning, he'd found the missing pink flip-flop in the sand, he told me. He was about to pick it up when he saw me in the water.

After a couple of hours, my mother said I was out of danger, and she offered us a ride. Nate and I sat in the backseat of my mother's gray sedan. ("Take a walk on the wild side," I'd pleaded when she bought it. "Get a blue car instead.")

When we reached the high school to drop off Nate, he gave me a long, warm hug while my mom pretended to fiddle with the radio. "I'll stop by later," he murmured. "After the time trials."

I nodded. I wasn't going anywhere.

At a stoplight (one of only three in town), my mother pulled out her cell phone. "Everything okay, there? I'll be home soon." She listened for a moment and then sighed. "I've rescheduled the appointment for tomorrow. We'll talk about it when I get home."

She folded up the phone and dropped it in her bag.

"What's Claire doing?" I asked from the backseat.

She was silent for a moment. "Thinking about how much she hates me," she said finally.

After she left me off, I punched *1-2-3-4-5* into the security panel and let myself in the front door. The Ice Cube House was empty. The Sealys were still at the hospital, along with Consuela, who was there to keep an eye on Cameron.

The last time I'd seen them, they were in the beach parking lot next to the ambulance. Prescott was on a stretcher. Mr. Sealy, wrapped in a heated blanket, knelt on the ground next to his son, sobbing, "I'm sorry, I'm sorry," while a paramedic tugged on his shoulder. "Sir, we have to check your vitals. Sir, we're doing all we can."

In the parking lot, Cameron grasped Consuela's hand, perfectly still, until Mrs. Sealy came running down the beach. When Cameron saw his mother, he ran to her and they collided. They clutched each other, gasping for air. For a moment, it was if they were the ones drowning, holding on to each other for their very survival.

Inside the Ice Cube House, I didn't even bother looking at the ocean before heading down the stairs to my airless room. For once, I was glad that it was dark in there. The scrubs made perfect pajamas. When I woke up, I would take a long bath. I would run conditioner through my wild hair and comb it until it shined.

I would call Nate. Surely the Sealys would let me see him. He had saved Prescott's life, after all.

Tomorrow I would start Larissa's body on an exercise program. I'd swim—a mile a day. Run a few times a week. Maybe I'd add a little weight training to the mix, put some muscle on these scrawny arms. Larissa's body would never be as powerful as mine, but you have to work with what you've got.

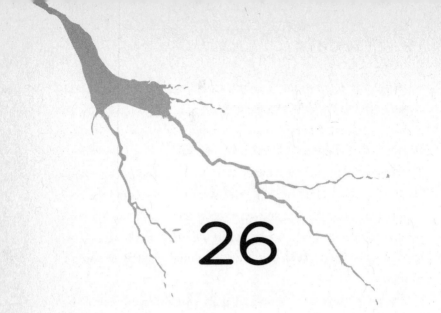

26

I COULDN'T BREATHE. Someone was suffocating me. I screamed and thrust my hands toward my face.

Yerowwwl!

I sat up in bed and stared at my cat. He shot me a look of pure disdain and then started licking his paw.

I played the day through my mind: the rescue, the clinic, the drive home with my mother. Had she taken me to our blue house? I couldn't remember.

And suddenly, I knew. I was me again.

"No!" I wailed to Fluffernutter. (He ignored me.) I wanted to see Nate later. I bounded out of bed and over to my mirror, expecting to see my regular self staring back. The red hair made me yelp.

"Evelyn?" I looked around the room: no apparition. She'd probably slipped over to peek in the neighbors' window again, or maybe she was busy hacking into my mother's computer. Out the window, I saw the briefest shadow of her, sitting on the front steps, smoking her ghostly cigarette.

On top of my dresser was a sand dollar, fresh grains still clinging to its face. Between loitering by Dumpsters and yapping with Roger, Evelyn must have squeezed in a little beachcombing. She always said sand dollars brought good luck. Maybe they did.

I peeked back at the mirror, at my wide-eyed face and that ridiculous hair. And then I burst out laughing. I was back. I was me. I checked the clock: If I hurried, I could make it to the pool in time.

I pulled on my Speedo and a pair of sweatpants (which, yes, I had found in the Sears boys' department). I felt warmer than I had in days.

Fluffernutter had settled himself back on my pillow. I leaned over, planted my face in his fur and inhaled. "I missed you, tuna breath."

Fluff said "yeow" and began to purr.

My mother was doing paperwork at the kitchen table, a cup of tea beside her.

"Time trials start in twenty minutes," I said. "Can you drive me?"

She stared at me for a moment and then nodded, tears glistening in her eyes. She stood up slowly. I hurried across the linoleum and grabbed her. She hugged me back.

"I love you, Mom."

"I don't understand—"

"You don't have to. I'm back."

She took a step back and looked me in the eyes. Tears were

197

streaming down her face. "We're still going tomorrow. To the doctor."

I nodded.

"We need to understand," she continued. "We can't let this happen again. It could be chemical; there are pharmaceuticals. We need to do tests, a CAT scan maybe, and—"

"Mom!" I interrupted. "We only have twenty minutes to get to the pool!"

When I walked into the swim center, I expected everyone to stare. There was that ridiculous red hair, after all. And I was late. And, let's be honest, I'd gotten used to people staring at me. The swimmers, parents, and coaches glanced up when the door slammed behind me, the sound echoing in the muggy, high-ceilinged room, but then they all went back to what they were doing: adjusting goggles, stretching muscles, checking lists.

Only one person stared at me, but she quickly looked away. I went right over to her. "Beanie, you're here!" She was wearing her red tank suit from sea-guard camp, a duffel bag at her feet.

She shrugged, looked at the tile floor. "Yeah. I'm not going to make it, but—whatever."

"You are so going to make it," I said. "Your backstroke rocks. And your breaststroke is really good too."

She shrugged.

"I'm sorry," I said. "About the way I've been acting."

"I should really warm up," she said to the floor.

"You have every right to be mad at me. But I'll make it up to you, I promise."

She looked me in the eye. "It's like you've become a totally different person."

"But I'm not!" I said. "It was just—it was an experiment. For social studies."

She shook her head. "You just don't get it." She turned and began to walk away.

"Jelly Bean, wait!"

She turned her head. "I have to get in the water. They're doing the backstroke trials first."

My mother sat on the bottom row of the bleachers, her face scrunched in concern. I took a few steps toward Beanie. "My mother is going to take me for a brain scan tomorrow," I murmured. "To see if there's something . . . in there." I put a hand on my forehead and blinked back tears that I was surprised to discover were real. I felt bad about manipulating Beanie like this, but then again, maybe there really was something wrong with my brain.

Beanie's eyes widened. "Oh, my God. I'm so sorry that I—"

I shook my head. "It's totally my fault."

"Is there anything I can do?"

I looked at the pool. People were jumping in and taking their positions in their lanes. "Yeah," I told her. "Get in that pool and swim faster than ever."

She made the team, of course, as did I. Not to brag, but my butterfly was just short of the school record. I probably could have beaten it if I'd been practicing for the last few days, but I had three years ahead of me.

The only bad part of the trials was Nate. At some level, I expected him to look deep into my eyes and recognize me.

Instead, he was just another one of the masses who glanced up when I came in the swim-center door, gave me a polite smile, and then looked away when he realized I was no one important.

After he swam the freestyle—easily clocking the fastest time—I padded over to him, my wide feet damp on the warm tiles. "Hey, Nate. Great form out there."

He grabbed a towel and rubbed his blond curls. "Thanks." He smiled at me: very nice, very friendly, very Nate. But it was nothing like the way he'd looked at me when I was Larissa. I remembered the emptiness I'd felt in my mom's kind, impersonal gaze when she'd seen me as Larissa. Why couldn't everyone love me no matter whose body I was in? If a person loves me, shouldn't he be able to see beyond my surface?

He ran a hand over his sea green eyes. His eyelashes were damp from the pool. He was beautiful. But that wasn't why I loved him, was it? Surely my feelings went deeper than that. I told myself I'd recognize him and love him no matter what he looked like, but the truth is—I don't know.

"Have you talked to Larissa today?" he asked me.

"Larissa?" I felt a stab of jealousy. "Just for a little while. She told me about the kid."

He nodded, and his eyes got this faraway look. "She was amazing."

"I heard you were the one who pulled him out of the water."

"Well, yeah. But I wouldn't have made it in time without her. She swam out there—it was really far—and she can barely swim!"

I felt irrationally irritated. He was talking about me, and yet he wasn't.

"By the way, she told me she was leaving today," I said. "She said to say good-bye."

I hadn't meant to hurt him, and yet I did. I had no idea when the real Larissa was leaving, of course; I just wanted to head off trouble.

"Did she leave a number?"

I shook my head. "She said you can e-mail her. You have her address?" I wasn't quite ready to let go of him. Not yet.

"Yeah—Rapunzel." A smile twitched at his lips. "I thought that was really cute."

I resisted the impulse to whip him with my wet towel, to yell, "Look at me! Don't you know who I am?"

Instead I smiled politely and said, "I guess Larissa is more than just a pretty face," before heading to the bleachers.

On the way, the coach stopped me and gave me a high five. "Lookin' good out there!"

I beamed.

His daughter Holly, a junior, came scurrying over. She'd swum the butterfly too, but had finished near the back of the pack. "Dad! I messed up!"

He chuckled and gave her a big hug. "Your start was a little rough. But you were going good at the end." He rubbed her wet hair.

"No! I stunk!" She grinned at me. "I'd give anything to have a butterfly like yours."

Anything? I looked at her dad, his hand still on Holly's damp head. If I had a father, I'd want him to be just like the coach.

"No, you wouldn't," I told Holly.

At the bleachers, I wrapped my towel around my waist and sat next to my mother. We waved good-bye to a mom we knew and a couple of dads. The swim center was emptying out. "I have something to ask you," I blurted.

"What?" She tensed her shoulders.

"Why did you get new carpet without asking me?" I'd chickened out from what I was going to say, but that carpet really did have to go.

She leaned back, relaxed. "I didn't think you'd care."

"I do care," I grumbled. "I hate the new carpet. It's, it's . . . beige. And polyester. And it smells funny."

"Okay."

"Can we rip it out? In my room, at least?"

She nodded. "If that will make you happy."

"It will. Oh, and Mom?"

"Yes?"

Say it. Just say it.

"Who's my father?" I kept my voice calm and casual, as if I were asking, "What's for dinner?" (A question she'd be more apt to ask *me*.)

She blinked nervously. "Is that what all of this"—she pointed at my hair—"is about?" Around us, voices bounced off the massive walls and high ceiling. Kids splashed in the pool. The air hung heavy with humidity and chlorine.

"Tell me."

She twisted the band on her left ring finger. It was silver with a green stone. She'd bought it for herself years before, after she'd grown tired of people checking to see if she was married.

"This is not the time or place I imagined having this discussion, but . . . okay." She took a deep breath. "His name was John."

There it was: the name I'd hungered for. John. So simple, so clear. John, John, John.

"I met him on a Tuesday in June," she told me. "In my office. A walk-in."

"You mean he was a patient?"

"Just that one time. He'd been surfing down at the point and stepped on a stingray. I pulled out the barb."

I shuddered. Everyone from around here knows to shuffle their feet around the point. It's got the best waves around, all things being relative, but also the highest concentration of stingrays.

"He was brave," she said. "Didn't yell or whimper or anything, just clenched his teeth and held his foot perfectly still. When the barb was finally out, he said, 'Actually, this was all just an excuse to spend some time with you.' That made me laugh." Her face softened. "Your grandfather had died the year before. I hadn't laughed in a long, long time."

She covered her face with her hands for a moment. Then, she cleared her throat and looked at me. "I've always tried to set a good example for you. Actions speak louder than words, you know, and—"

"Finish the story," I said.

She nodded. "I had the next day off. I worked Saturdays then, so Wednesdays, I was free. I went to the beach."

"You never go to the beach," I said.

"I did when I was younger. Plus . . ."

"You hoped to run into him." I pictured myself sitting on a beach towel, pretending to appreciate the scenery when, really, I was searching for Nate.

She nodded. "I liked him. And, he was quite good-looking—tall and athletic, with dark hair and these grayish green eyes. And he had a dimple in his chin. Like you. Of course, I wasn't sure he'd ever go in the water again, after the stingray, but there he was."

Had he been looking for her too? I wondered. Maybe he was plotting to "accidentally" twist an ankle in a child's abandoned hole or cut his finger on a shell.

"He recognized me right away," she said. "Even without the white coat. And we got to talking. He was from up north. He'd just gotten a graduate degree in architecture, and he was traveling around the country before deciding where to settle down."

She grew quiet.

"How long did he stay?" I prodded, hungry for details.

"Just till that Saturday." She shot me a sheepish look. "I called in sick Thursday and Friday."

My jaw dropped. My mother never calls in sick, even when she can barely get out of bed.

"He never promised me anything," she said in a rush. "And I never expected anything in return. We were just . . . in the moment. Collecting seashells, wandering through the farmers' market. Making dinner together and laughing. Always laughing."

"You *cooked?*" That was almost more shocking than a fling with a stranger.

"Okay, he cooked," she admitted. "I watched. Plus I did some of the chopping." She paused, and her eyes grew happy and sad all at once, with a distant look, as if she were watching a memory long buried.

"I was sad when he left," she told me. "And, of course, a part of me kept hoping he'd come back. But mostly I was grateful for the time we had together. He showed me I could be happy again."

"But you were pregnant," I said.

"Indeed I was." She blushed.

"Just like Chastity Dunhauser." I couldn't help it: It just slipped out.

She straightened. "But with a medical degree. And a means of supporting myself." Her mouth twitched. "But, okay—kind of like Chastity Dunhauser."

"Did you tell him? About me?" I was almost afraid to hear the answer.

She shook her head. "At first, I didn't think he needed to know. But then, after you were born, I thought he might want to see you. Plus, I figured you'd start asking questions when you got older."

Actually, I'd started asking questions from the time I was old enough to talk.

"So I checked the files at the clinic," she said. "But the only address he had given was his local hotel, and he hadn't filled in his social security number."

"What about a last name?" I asked.

She smiled ruefully. "Smith."

"John Smith." I swallowed. "Great." I remembered what she'd said about the architecture studies. "But he'd just gotten a degree, right? Couldn't you check with the university?"

"I tried that." She held my eyes for a moment before looking away. "They had no record of him."

I let this information sink in. "So he lied about going to school?"

She hesitated. "He definitely lied about something."

John Smith. Why not just call himself John Doe? "So maybe that wasn't even his real name." In which case I'd never know who he was. Never.

She nodded and took my hand. "I know how it sounds, but I've never regretted it, not for an instant. He made me want to live again. Besides, I got *you* out of the whole deal, and you're the best thing that's ever happened to me." She ran a hand along my wet hair. "I should have told you sooner. But I didn't know how to explain that you can love someone you barely know, even if you're not entirely sure who he is. And that you hold on to that love and find joy in it long after he's gone. I don't expect you to understand. I don't entirely understand it myself."

"But I do understand," I whispered. "I understand more than you can know."

27

MY MOTHER SAID I could go to the snack shack with Beanie. She was worried, I could tell, but she loved Beanie, and she knew that Beanie was good for me.

Beanie called her mom to tell her about the swim team and to ask if she could have dinner with me. "The snack shack. With Claire. I don't know—a salad or something. I won't get the onion rings. . . . I know, Mother. I *know*."

She closed her phone and blinked back tears. "Do they still have those veggie burgers at the snack shack?"

I shook my head. "No one ever ordered them."

"Why not?"

"Because they tasted like dirt." I was trying to make her smile. It didn't work. "You know, Beanie, training in the pool two hours a day—it's not like splashing around at sea camp. You're going to work your butt off. You'll be starving pretty much all of the time."

"Great," she moaned.

I shook my head. "You can eat anything, and you'll still lose weight! Not that you need to. Forget what your mother says."

She nodded like she didn't believe me. "Maybe I'll get a chicken sandwich." She checked her duffel bag to make sure she had her wallet. "At practice yesterday? I brought my stuff in a beach bag. I looked like a complete dork."

"Nah," I said. "I bet no one even noticed."

"Oh, and I saw Nate with that blond girl, you know the one we saw at the beach?" She zipped the bag and straightened. "I talked to them for a little bit."

"Really?" I said casually. "What's she like?"

Beanie shuddered. "A total bitch."

"Maybe she's not so bad when you get to know her." I was feeling bad for having judged Larissa so harshly.

She swung her head to look at me. "You're kidding, right?"

I remembered the way I'd treated Beanie: the eye rolling, the stuff with the Snickers bar. "Of course I'm kidding. C'mon, let's get out of here."

At the beach, my mother sat in her car watching us cross the parking lot to the snack shack. "I'm fine!" I called to her. "I'll be home in an hour."

She frowned with concern and then turned the car back on. "I love you," she called out. To my surprise, I wasn't even embarrassed (though I'd wait till I got home to tell her that I loved her too).

Alexei was at the counter. With all the kids back in school, they'd run out of fluent English speakers to take orders. Not that it mattered: Anyone with a fifty-word vocabulary (burger, shake, dog, fries—you get the picture) could succeed at the snack shack.

I approached first (Beanie was trying to decide between a grilled-chicken sandwich and a turkey burger). "I'll have a foot-long dog. And a Sprite." I really wanted a bacon cheeseburger and a shake, but I didn't want to torture Beanie.

"Wiv zuh dog, you want zuh everything?" Alexei's face was all seriousness.

"Yeah, the everything. I mean, everything." That meant jalapeños, onions, and pickles. Good thing I wouldn't be kissing Nate tonight. Yeah, real good thing.

Alexei nodded and wrote my order—in slow, spiky letters—on a green order pad.

"I didn't think you'd still be here," I said. "Are you staying in the United States?"

He shook his head. "I haff work permit—is for summer, just. I leaf, it is in two days."

"But you come back next summer, maybe?"

He glanced at Beanie, who quickly looked away. "I don't know. But I like that. I like that berry, berry much."

I stepped aside to make room for Beanie. "What's better?" she asked Alexei. "The chicken sandwich or the turkey burger?"

He shook his head. "Is neither. Is best is the cheeseburger. You get?"

She scrunched up her nose. "Too fattening."

"Ugh!" Alexei threw back his head. "You American girls, you think too much about is fattening! American girls, so many is too skinny, is all bones! But you—" He looked at Beanie intently. "You is perfect."

209

They stared at each other over the counter. Her face flushed red, her eyes shone.

Alexei put his elbows on the counter and leaned forward. "You have cheeseburger, yes?"

"Yes," she whispered in a husky voice.

"And onion rings?"

"Yes."

"And—I think a shake? Is chocolate?"

"Oh, yes!" She caught herself. "On second thought, I'll just have water. Wouldn't want to overdo."

When the food came, I went to the counter to get my hot dog and soda. Alexei slid the cheeseburger across the counter to Beanie (I could have gotten my bacon cheeseburger, after all). She reached for the ketchup. He grabbed her hand.

"I do for you," he said. He pulled the burger bun off. With the red plastic ketchup bottle, he drew a heart on top of Beanie's cheeseburger.

"Oh, wow," she murmured.

"Catch you later," I whispered in Beanie's ear. She nodded without taking her eyes off of Alexei.

I started down the road, eating as I walked, until I reached the street that led to the beach houses. They looked different from the road: far less impressive and more like regular old houses—or, worse, like a great, big line of garages. Trash day was tomorrow; the curb was cluttered with green garbage cans.

Outside the Ice Cube House, the pink flip-flop was in the second can I opened, sitting on top of a tied black trash bag. I pulled it out with two fingers, half expecting it to be covered with something sticky or slimy or smelly. But it was just the way I had left it, white sand still clinging to the crevices.

The front door banged open. I crammed the flip-flop into the front pocket of my red lifeguard hoodie.

She was wearing the white sundress, her blond hair pulled back in a ponytail. She carried a tropical-print duffel bag over to a worn but clean-looking tan SUV. A man followed her out the door. Even from this distance, I could tell it wasn't Mr. Sealy. This guy was taller and thinner, and he wore a faded blue T-shirt that Mr. Sealy wouldn't be caught dead in. It was the man in the photograph. It was Larissa's father.

I licked my finger and rubbed it around my mouth to remove any traces of mustard. Slowly, carefully, holding my breath, I approached the SUV. Larissa and her father looked up at the same time.

"Hi," I said.

"Howdy," Larissa's father said. I liked that. He went back to packing the SUV—a couple of shopping bags, a laundry basket.

"I'm Claire," I said to Larissa.

Her eyes grew huge. She shot a glance at her father and then walked with me to the end of the driveway.

"So it was real?" she whispered.

I nodded. It was hard not to stare. She seemed more beautiful than ever: more vibrant than when I'd first seen her on the beach, less self-conscious than when I'd first seen her face reflected in the mirror. Never underestimate the power of a few days in the sun and a whole lot of onion rings.

She blinked, confused. "For a while I thought I was dreaming.

And then I thought I was dead. There was this angel with red hair. . . ."

"I don't know that I'd call her an angel," I said. "A spirit, maybe."

"Are you a spirit too?"

"Me? Oh, no! I'm just a normal—well, I'm just a person. So, do you . . . remember everything?"

She pulled her ponytail forward and played with the end. "Not much. Just a few pieces here and there. I remember pink pills. And sleeping. Then I was kind of floating, up by the ceiling. I saw you go out of the room, and then later you came back. And there was this lady—I guess it was your mom. She looked worried. And this girl walked in."

Here she froze for a moment. When she started speaking again, her voice was soft, almost hoarse. "It was me—the girl. She looked just like me. That's when I thought I was dead."

I looked back at her father. He smiled at us.

"You were never dead," I said. "You just . . . became part of a greater whole for a while. We're all connected, in a way. Only most of the time, we don't know it. Does that make sense?"

She considered. "No."

"It's probably best if you don't mention this to anyone," I said.

She nodded. "Nobody would believe me anyway."

"Just so you know," I said. "I didn't mean for this to happen. I mean, I didn't do it on purpose."

She smiled a little. "It's okay. It worked out in the end."

Her father was arranging things in the back of the SUV. "Your dad seems nice."

"He is. I still can't believe he's here."

"I sent him an e-mail," I told her. "You know . . . from you." Was there anything else she needed to know? "Oh! And you saved a kid from drowning yesterday. If anyone mentions it, just smile and nod."

"But I can't even swim!"

"It's all in the mind. Trust me. So . . . it's okay? The custody and everything?"

She tossed her ponytail behind her shoulder. "The lawyers still have to fight over the details, but yeah, we'll get a lot more time together. He talked to my mother this morning. Her ship was in, like, Crete or something. She knew she was busted. She said me and my dad could be together till she gets back."

"I'm really happy for you." I put my hands in the pocket of my hoodie and touched rubber. I pulled out the flip-flop. "I almost forgot. I lost the other one on the beach. I'm really sorry."

"Don't worry about it." She shrugged. "I never liked them much anyway. A little too girly, ya know?"

I slipped the shoe back into my pocket.

Larissa's father closed the back of the SUV and strode over. He put his arm around Larissa and kissed the top of her head. He looked like her: same mud-colored eyes, same straight nose, same oval-shaped face. His lips were thinner, though, and the pieces didn't fit together quite the same way. Genetics are a funny thing.

"Say good-bye to your cat for me," Larissa said.

"I will."

"You're lucky you're not allergic," she said. "And from what I could see, you're lucky about a lot of things."

I nodded. She was right.

28

I RAN INTO NATE AT THE END OF THE ROAD.

"Dude," he said, his eyes searching. "Is she still here?"

I shook my head. "You just missed her." It was true: The tan SUV had passed a minute earlier.

Nate's face fell. He stuck his hands into his red hoodie (we matched) and pulled out a pink flip-flop, the mate to the one in my own front pocket.

"I was going to give her this," he said.

"I'll take it," I said, reaching for the shoe. "She gave me the other one to hold on to. You know, in case this one ever showed up."

The rubber flip-flop felt surprisingly warm, almost magical. The pink and orange petals at the V matched the clouds that framed the setting sun. The storm had never made it to land, but the clouds painted a spectacular sunset.

I reached into my pocket and pulled out the other shoe, and then I dropped them both onto the sandy street.

I kicked off one sneaker and then another.

"Do you think they'd fit me?"

He gazed at the shoes.

"It's funny." He tilted his head back up. His eyes were so green. "I wouldn't have guessed that you and Larissa would wear the same size, but they look like they'd be perfect." With the sun behind him, his golden curls glowed orange at the edges. He looked like an angel.

"Try them on," he said, smiling. "I think they'd look good on you."

In the rosy glow of the sunset, on that cool and sandy street, I took a deep breath and stepped into the pink shoes.